M

I

J

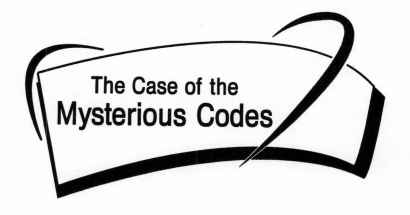

The Case of the
Mysterious Codes

The Case of the
Mysterious Codes

THE **KeRRy** HILL

CASECRACKERS

by
John F. Warner
and Peggy Nicholson

Lerner Publications Company / Minneapolis

Cover art by Christopher Nick

Library of Congress Cataloging-in-Publication Data

Nicholson, Peggy.
    The case of the mysterious codes / by John F. Warner and
Peggy Nicholson.
        p.   cm. — (Kerry Hill Casecrackers ; #4)
    Summary: Jason and the new friends he and his sister have
made during their summer in Newport, Rhode Island, try to
figure out the coded messages he has been getting from a
mysterious stranger.
    ISBN 0-8225-0712-9 :
    [1. Mystery and detective stories. 2. Ciphers — Fiction.]
I. Warner, J. F. (John F.) II. Title. III. Series: Nicholson, Peggy.
Kerry Hill Casecrackers ; #4.
PZ7.N5545Caq 1995
[Fic]—dc20   94-8532
                                                                CIP
                                                                 AC

Manufactured in the United States of America

1 2 3 4 5 6 — I/BP — 00 99 98 97 96 95

CONTENTS

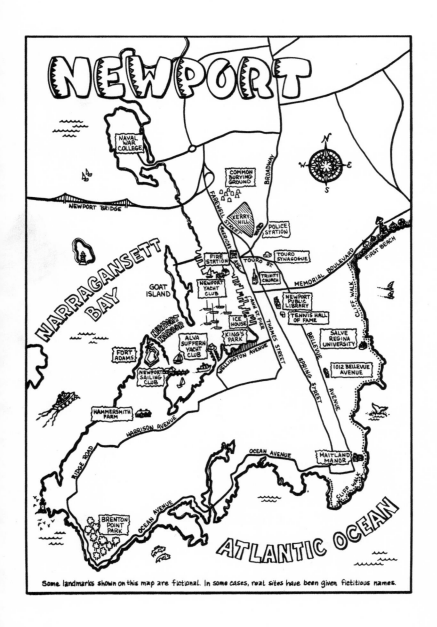

Some landmarks shown on this map are fictional. In some cases, real sites have been given fictitious names.

THE MASKED RIDER

"You're very brave, leaving Eddie to watch Jason," Tuyet giggled as she followed Hally up the outside stairs to the Watkins's deck. "I bet they're fighting."

Hally's eight-year-old brother, Jason, loved to tease, and their friend Eddie Machado had a quick temper.

"I bet they're eating peanut butter and something horrible on bread," Hally countered. "And what else could I do? I promised I'd help you rearrange your room, and Jason wouldn't come with me. So when Eddie stopped by, I dumped Jason on him and ran."

The two friends hurried across the shady second-story deck, then in through the screen door to the Watkins's kitchen.

WHUMP! Thumpety-Thump-THUMP! "What's that?" Tuyet peered down the hallway toward the bedrooms.

"Lemme out, you lousy little shrimp," yelled Eddie, his voice muffled. "Or I'll—" The thumping started again.

The commotion was coming from the bathroom. Jason stood outside the door, his head cocked to one side, his brown cowlick standing on end. He turned and grinned at Hally. "He sure is mad."

"You bet I'm mad!" Eddie howled. "And if you don't unlock the door *this minute,* I'm gonna kick it from here to Nantucket!"

"Eddie, I'm here!" Hally called. "Calm down and we'll get you out." She glared at her brother. "Where's the key?" Usually, a big iron key stayed in the keyhole on the inside of the bathroom door. Jason must have taken it, then locked Eddie in from the outside.

Jason smirked. "Someplace safe."

"There ain't gonna be anyplace safe this side of the moon if you don't get me that key!" Eddie raged through the door.

"Eddie, give me a minute," Hally pleaded. She glared at her little brother. "Okay, Jase, what's the story?"

"I'm proving my theory," Jason said. "I'm proving that Eddie's the one who's been sending me the black codes."

Mysterious coded messages had been arriving all summer, each of them addressed to "Mr. Jason Watkins, Esquire." They were all printed in jagged silver letters on black paper, and each code was more difficult than the last. All of the codes had been dropped in the Watkins's mailbox—but not by the mail carrier, since they were never stamped or postmarked.

"I've got better things to do than send you

codes. Like I'm gonna send you a knuckle sandwich, if you don't get that key!" Eddie roared.

"Eddie can't be sending you the messages," Tuyet reasoned in her soft voice. "He's a Kerry Hill Casecracker, just like the rest of us. Casecrackers solve mysteries, they don't make them."

The Kerry Hill Casecrackers were Joe Kerry, Eddie Machado, Nguyen Tuyet, and Jason and Hally Watkins. Joe and Eddie were natives of Newport, Rhode Island. Tuyet had come here years ago from Vietnam to live with her aunt and uncle. Jason and Hally were summer visitors. Best friends now, they all had met each other and banded together at the start of the summer.

When Tuyet had been accused of burning down a house, they had proved her innocent. Next the Casecrackers had solved the mystery of a ghost that haunted the lighthouse on Hazard Island. Then only a few weeks ago, they had helped catch a burglar who had been stealing antiques from Maitland Manor.

"The only mystery to me is how that shrimp has managed to live so long!" Eddie yelled. He kicked the door.

"Last month you thought it was Aiden who was sending you the codes," Hally reminded her brother. They had met Aiden Hallisey when they were investigating the Hazard Island lighthouse. "And then you thought it was Tuyet or me."

Jason stuck out his bottom lip and looked stubborn. "So it's gotta be Eddie. Or if it isn't, we'll know anytime now."

"Know what?" asked Joe Kerry as he ambled down the hallway. He pulled off his gold, wire-rimmed glasses and smiled at Hally while he cleaned them on his T-shirt. "I did knock," he said, "but nobody heard me." At thirteen, Joe was the oldest of the Casecrackers by months, and the tallest by several lanky inches. With his sun-bleached blond hair, he looked like a surfer, though he spent as much time in the library as he did at the beach.

"Joe, you're here? Would you get me *out?*" Eddie yelled.

"Jason's proving that Eddie has been sending the codes," Hally explained. "Or that he hasn't," she added, looking at Jason. "What did you mean by that—that we'll know anytime now?"

Jason smirked. "Didn't anybody but me notice the pattern? The codes always come on a Monday or on a Friday. Today's Friday. So if a code doesn't come, it's because Eddie couldn't deliver it. But if a code does come while he's locked up, that proves he's innocent."

"Unless he meant to deliver it on a Monday this time," Joe pointed out, laughing. "You plan to keep him locked up till Monday?"

"He's not keeping me here another ten minutes!" Eddie hollered.

"No, he's not," Hally agreed. "Jason, go get the key *right now!*"

Jason crossed his arms and shook his head. Hally let out a hiss. Jason had to be the most stubborn person she had ever known!

"If you guys won't get me out, then I'm gonna burn down this door," Eddie said. "I've got matches. And plenty of towels and paper. See if I don't!"

"Wouldn't it be simpler if we just took the door off its hinges?" Joe suggested calmly. He dug in his pocket and produced a Swiss Army knife. He flipped out a screwdriver-shaped blade. "I'll pop the pins. Have you out in no time, Ed. Stay cool."

"Eddie isn't sending you the codes," Tuyet told Jason, while Joe pried at the bottom hinge pin. "The Casecrackers should be working together to catch the one who brings them. He might be on your front porch right now, dropping the next code in the mailbox."

Jason shook his head. "What do you think, I'm dumb or something? I took care of that too. I rigged a bell to the box. If anybody lifts the lid—" His head swung toward the living room windows. Everyone froze.

The sound Jason had heard came again. *Ting-tingle-ting!*

"That's it!" Jason shrieked. "That's my bell!" He raced for the front room, with the other Casecrackers stampeding behind him.

"Hey!" Eddie yelled, but no one stopped to explain.

Hally joined Jason, who leaned halfway out the window that overlooked the front porch. Tuyet nudged in beside them. Joe hung out the window over the couch. The roof of the porch had been torn down years ago, so they had a clear view of the mailbox.

One floor below, a man stood frozen. He was dressed all in black, from his sweatshirt to his baggy pants. He had lifted the mailbox lid with a gloved hand and was peering into it. *Trying to figure out what the bell is*, Hally guessed. Just then, the figure looked up, and she gasped. He was wearing a black ski mask! She couldn't see any part of his face, except for a pair of dark eyes gazing straight up at her!

"Hold it right there!" Jason yelled. He ducked away, then returned and dropped a coil of rope onto the porch. The man sidestepped the rope, but still stared upward.

"You just hold it right there, Mister!" Jason's rope dangled out the window, all the way to the porch floor. Inside the house, Jason had tied it to a leg of the couch. Now he squirmed out onto the windowsill, and gripped the rope with both hands.

The man lifted a long arm and pointed his finger at Jason. He shook his masked head slowly and sternly. *No!* his gesture said, as clearly as if he'd spoken aloud.

"No!" Hally agreed. She grabbed Jason's belt just as he started to slither off the sill. "No way are you sliding down that rope!"

"Then how else am I s'posed to catch him!" Jason yelled, his face turning red and his feet kicking. "Lemme go, Hally!"

"He's going anyway. You'd never catch him." The man wheeled around and bounded down the porch steps to a black mountain bike that leaned on its kickstand nearby. As he mounted the bike, Hally heard the sound of running footsteps.

The mysterious figure heard them too. He stomped on the pedals, and the bike tore across the sidewalk. It bumped over the curb, then shot down the street—just as Joe and Tuyet burst around the corner of the house. They staggered to a halt and watched, panting, as man and bike receded in the distance. As he turned the corner, the rider looked back, and swung his arm in a wide wave.

"What the heck's going on?" Eddie howled from the bathroom.

"I s'pose I've gotta let him out now," Jason said with regret, as he wriggled back over the windowsill. "You wouldn't maybe..."

Hally snorted. "Let him out for you? Not on

your life!" While Jason trudged off to retrieve the key and Joe and Tuyet straggled upstairs, Hally went to the freezer. She pulled out a carton of ice cream.

When Jason unlocked the door, his prisoner stormed out. Hally stepped between them and held up a tablespoon before Eddie's pug nose. "You have to eat ten spoonfuls before you kill him." She shoved the open carton into his hands, then the spoon.

Eddie scowled, switching his gaze from the carton of chocolate chip ice cream to Jason, then back to the carton. "You have to," Hally insisted. "And while you do, we'll fill you in."

By the fourth bite, Eddie's freckled face was turning from strawberry pink back to its normal tan. "But I'll recognize that bike if I ever see it again," Joe said. "A black, custom jobbie. And where the license plate would be on a car..." He paused dramatically.

"Yeah?" Eddie growled.

"A playing card! Couldn't get close enough to see which one. It wasn't a face card, but it was one of the red suits—either a heart or diamond."

"Weird!" Eddie agreed. He let out a long sigh, then pried an extra-large chunk of chocolate from a slope of vanilla. He flicked a keen glance at Jason, who stood down the hall, ready to bolt outside if need be.

"Tuyet and I saved this till you could see it," Joe told Hally. From his pocket, he drew out a familiar black envelope with silver jagged letters on its front.

"Hey, that's for me!" Jason yelped, as Joe handed the message to Hally.

"It is," she agreed. "But first, what do you say to Eddie?"

Jason made a face. "Sorry," he mumbled.

Joe and Hally each cupped a hand to one ear. "What?" they sang. Tuyet giggled and did the same. Eddie started to grin.

"Sorry." Jason growled a little louder and shuffled his feet.

"WHAAAAT?" everyone cried.

"I'm SORRY!" Jason hollered, dancing with impatience. "SORRY, SORRY, SORRY, SORRY! Are you satisfied? Now give me my blasted code!"

"Better give it to him before he pops," Eddie said, laughing.

Scowling, Jason ripped open the envelope. He pulled out a folded black paper, and as he did, something light brown and knobby fell to the floor. He stooped, reached for it, and froze. "Yow!"

"What is it?" Hally asked, kneeling beside him.

"Yow-sa-mighty!" Jason picked the thing up by one end. He shook it, and it made a dry-bones, whispery clicking. "It's a *rattlesnake* tail!" He looked thrilled and frightened at the same time.

"I don't like this!" Hally muttered. "Who've you made so mad?" Or who, come to think of

19

it, had Jason *not* made mad since he arrived in Newport?

"Who knows?" Jason shook the rattle next to his ear.

"And where's the rest of the snake?" Tuyet wondered.

"Maybe that's what he'll bring you next time," Eddie said, not smiling now.

"Something really weird is going on here," Joe said solemnly. "And I think the Casecrackers should get to the bottom of this—the case of the mysterious codes!"

CHAPTER 2

STUYVESANT THE SNOB

"Two mysteries in one day!" Tuyet murmured blissfully, a short while later. The Casecrackers sat on the town pier, kicking their heels over the water. Below them, Eddie crouched in his dinghy, *Netop*, while he bailed out last night's rainwater.

"You're going to love this one," Joe promised. The Casecrackers had someplace to go, and something very important to do, he'd announced mysteriously back at the Watkins's apartment.

Whatever it was, Eddie was in on the secret. He'd said that they would go by water to where they were going.

So they had temporarily set aside the mystery of Jason's codes. At least everyone but Jason had set it aside. Hally's little brother sat beside her on the pier, squinting down at his latest code, and emitting a series of tiny grunts as he thought about it. Judging from Jason's sound effects, this one would be a monster to crack.

Sam, Joe's big golden retriever, was worried by Jason's sounds. Tail waving anxiously, he strolled over and stuck his tongue in Jason's ear.

"Errk! Stupid dog." Jason shoved him aside without looking up.

"Ready," Eddie called.

The Casecrackers scrambled into their usual places in the dinghy. Tuyet and Joe sat in the bow, or front, and Eddie took the rowing position on the middle seat. Hally and Jason sat in the stern, with Sam crouched on the floorboards between Eddie's legs.

Tuyet shoved the bow out from the dock. Eddie dipped his oars into the water and started rowing. The dinghy glided out past the long piers, with their big, shiny motor yachts tied alongside, out into Newport Harbor.

Out on the moorings, hundreds of sailboats and powerboats bobbed and nodded with the waves. A motor launch worked its way across the harbor, carrying passengers toward Fort Adams on the far side of the port. Seagulls wheeled and screeched overhead.

"So tell us the mystery," Tuyet pleaded. "Where are we going?"

Joe pointed across the water, where a white building sat in isolated splendor on a small rocky island. A long pier connected it to the far shore. "To the Alva Suffern Yacht Club."

"The snootiest place in all of Newport," Eddie added between oar strokes. "Snob city for sailors."

Hally brushed a wisp of light brown hair from her eyes. "Then why go there?"

"'Cause the club holds a crazy race at the

end of the summer," Joe explained. "Eddie and I have raced in it the last two years, but neither of us has ever placed. This year I think the Casecrackers should enter. If we put our heads together, I bet we can win."

Jason folded his code and put it away. "What's a crazy race?"

"It's a race where you have to build a boat—or anything that'll float and can be sailed. Then you put it in the water. First boat to cross the finish line wins," Joe said.

"You've got exactly two hours to build your boat," Eddie added, leaning back as he pulled on the oars. "You've got to be under sixteen to enter the race, and you can't have any grown-ups help in planning or building your entry. And no motors—it's got to move by wind."

"And you can't spend more than twenty-five dollars on materials," said Joe. "You ought to see some of the entries! Half of 'em sink in the first five minutes of the race. Somebody always tries to float one of those old bathtubs."

"Last year a kid used an old Volkswagen Bug with a mast mounted on the bumper," Eddie recalled. "It tipped over and sank."

"Sounds like great fun," Hally agreed. "Who won it last year?"

Eddie and Joe made faces. "Same guy who won it the year before that, and the year before that! B. Stuyvesant Van Zandt the Fourth," Eddie growled.

"No, really!" Hally laughed.

"He means it," Joe said. "Stuyvesant's the richest kid in all of Newport, if not all Rhode Island."

"And a sneaky cheat," Eddie said. "Just tell me that boat of his last year wasn't designed by a real naval architect!"

"And it cost a heap more than twenty-five dollars," Joe agreed.

"But if those are the rules?" Tuyet wondered.

Eddie shrugged. "Who's going to prove it,

Tuyet, and how? Besides, his dad is commodore of the yacht club. You don't think they bend the rules a bit for the head hot dog's baby boy?"

"But if he's got the money, we've got the brains," Joe said. "And a super skipper—Eddie's the best waterman in Newport. So let's not worry about Stuyvesant the Snob, let's worry about how to design a go-fast boat in seven days. 'Cause the race is next Saturday."

"And today's the last day to sign up," Eddie said.

As they drew nearer the gleaming white yacht club, Hally could see that rows of docks floated in the shelter of the granite island. Sleek sailboats and dinghys were tied bow to stern along the docks. "Wow, it's crowded, isn't it? How will we get ashore?"

"We'll just raft up," Eddie said, "like you'd double-park a car." He brought the dingy in gently next to a glossy, dark blue sailboat.

"Umm, don't you think we should pick on

somebody else?" Joe suggested, as Eddie shipped the oar nearest the boat.

Eddie grinned. "Not particularly." Careful not to bump the gleaming side of the sailboat, he caught hold of its rigging. "Ready with the bow line?"

Before Joe could answer, a boy's head rose up out of the sailboat's hatch. "What do you think you're doing?" He stepped up into the boat's cockpit, and stood glaring down at the Case-crackers. A second boy rose into view, then joined him on deck.

"Rafting up for a few minutes," Eddie said. "We've got to sign up for—"

"You're not scuffing up *my* topsides, townie!" said the first boy, who was dressed all in white. His shorts had an ironed crease in each leg. His shirt had curvy initials embroidered in navy blue above the pocket. "So shove off."

Eddie's face turned pink. "Now, look—"

"Look, Stuyvesant," Joe cut in. "Everyone

knows it's common courtesy to let someone raft up when there's no room to land."

The blond boy looked down his long nose at Joe. "You're going to give me a lesson in manners, Kerry? At my own club?"

"Not about to," Joe said mildly. "You're past teaching."

"Got 'im!" Jason crowed, as Stuyvesant's face turned a patchy pink. "You got him good, Joe!" He pounded gleefully on Sam's furry side. The big retriever had risen to his feet. He was waving his tail, eager to go ashore.

"Look," said Hally, "Why don't we just—"

"Get your hands off my boat, Machado!" snapped Stuyvesant. "You and your townie friends can tie off by the garbage cans, over there—*Hey!*" he yelped, as Sam leaped onto his sailboat.

At least Sam *tried* to leap onto the sailboat. His front half landed on the deck, and his back paws scrabbled at the boat's glossy hull as he tried to heave himself aboard. "My topsides!" shrieked Stuyvesant. "Scratch my topsides, you lousy mutt and I'll—" Grabbing Sam by the scruff of his neck, Stuyvesant heaved him over the dinghy!

"*Hey!*" everyone in the dinghy yelled, as Sam hit the water.

"I've got him!" Hally cried. Sam blinked his big brown eyes and looked bewildered. Hally caught his collar and held his head above water.

"If my dog's hurt, Van Zandt—" Joe's voice cracked with rage.

"If your mutt hurt my topsides, you'll pay for a new paint job." Stuyvesant leaned over to examine the hull.

"There's not a mark on it," Eddie growled. He shoved off from the sailboat. "Hold Sam's head up while I row," he ordered Hally. "We'll tow him ashore."

"Here's a scratch!" cried Stuyvesant, still leaning over the side.

"That's just mud," said Jason. "Lemme wash it off for you." He dipped the dinghy's half-gallon bailing scoop into the water. Then he splashed its entire contents over Stuyvesant's blond head! "Ooops! I missed. Sorry!" he giggled.

Stuyvesant let out of a howl of rage and stood up. "You little—" he sputtered. "Why, you little— I'm going to—"

"No, *we're* going to!" Hally glared up at him. "We're going to beat you fair and square, you stuck-up snob. In the crazy race. That's a promise!" The boats drew apart as Eddie steered the dinghy toward the next dock and a small open space beneath the bow of a powerboat.

Stuyvesant wiped the dripping hair out of his eyes, and let out a jeering laugh. "Oh, yeah, townie girl? Well, don't count on it!"

"But that's just what I'm doing," Hally swore, turning away from him to meet the angry eyes of her friends. Everyone nodded fierce agreement. "I'm counting on us. The Casecrackers are going to beat that snob if it's the last thing we ever do!"

Paddling alongside the dinghy, Sam snorted and shook his head.

"See?" said Jason. "Even Sam agrees. We're gonna beat that creep!"

CHAPTER 3

"AND SOMETIMES I'VE ET THEM"

"You see, you pull off their little...what-do-you-call-em...beards." Tuyet pulled the stringy stuff from the shell of a mussel. She and her uncle Chau-Li had gathered the shellfish that morning from the rocks off Brenton Reef. She'd brought the Watkinses a bucketful, and now she was showing Hally how to cook them. "Then you scrub each one." She placed the mussel in a bowl on the counter.

"I ain't gonna eat any of those," Jason announced from the table, where he sat working on his latest code. "Anything that hard on the outside is gonna be real gooshy on the inside.

I'd rather eat fried worms or asparagus."

"Fine," said Hally, as she pulled off a beard. "Dad and I will eat steamed mussels, and I'll cook you some worms. But *you* have to catch 'em." She grinned sideways at Tuyet. After living with and looking after Jason since the beginning of the summer, Hally was finally learning how to handle him.

It hadn't been easy. When he'd arrived in June to stay with Hally and their dad, Jason had been almost a stranger—and a grouchy, bad-tempered little stranger at that.

After their parents divorced, Jason and Hally had continued living in Houston, Texas. They had shuttled back and forth between their parents' homes. But then, three years ago, their mother took a job teaching school on an American army base in Germany. Hally hadn't liked having to choose between her parents, but finally she'd decided to stay in Houston. That's where her friends were, after all.

But at five years old, Jason couldn't bear to be parted from their mother. So he'd gone to Germany. He and Marti Watkins had moved back to the States several months ago. But this time, they settled in Iowa, where Mrs. Watkins was teaching at a small college.

Once the school year ended, Jason had come to Newport, since that's where Hally and their dad were staying for the summer. Then this winter, Hally would spend school vacations in Iowa.

"Have you cracked the code yet?" Tuyet asked.

"Not yet," Jason admitted. "But I'm close."

"What about his Viper letters?" Tuyet asked Hally, under cover of the running water. "Has he sent any more of them to the...the Hyena?" She giggled at the name.

Hally made a face. "He snuck out and mailed another last week."

Jason had been mad when he first arrived. He was convinced that he'd been sent to Newport not to visit, but so he'd be out of the way—to allow a man he called the Hyena to court and marry their mother.

The Hyena's real name was Hiram Abrams. He was a professor at the same college where their mother taught. According to Jason, he had red hair, too many freckles, and a big, goofy laugh like a hyena. And he was crazy about their mother.

But just because he'd been sent half the country away, Jason wasn't about to give up and let the Hyena win their mother without a fight. In spite of Hally's efforts to stop him, he'd been sending the professor weird, threatening letters and phone messages all summer. The messages warned that the Viper was coming—in six weeks. Then five weeks. Then four. His latest letter had warned that the Viper would be there in three weeks.

Jason never signed his threats, and he insisted that the Hyena was too dumb to figure out who sent them. Hally wasn't so sure.

"Ha!" Jason put down his pencil. "Got ya, Masked Rider!"

Hally and Tuyet dried their hands and went to see.

"See?" said Jason. "Each time he builds on the last code. Here's the key to the last one." He set a paper before them.

"I remember," said Tuyet. "A equals *1*, B equals *2*, and so on."

"Right. But this time, he got cute." Jason took his pencil and drew a line to cut the alphabet in two. "Now the alphabet's got twenty-six letters, right? Here's the middle, right between the thirteenth and fourteenth letters—*M* and *N*. So what if you turned everything inside out from the middle?" He drew an arrow pointing from the *M* to the *A*. Then he drew a second arrow pointing from the *N* to the *Z*. "See?" As the girls frowned at his diagram, not getting it, he started printing a second key on another sheet of paper. When he finished, he handed it to Hally. "So that gives you this."

A	B	C	D	E	F	G	H	I	J	K	L	M
13	12	11	10	9	8	7	6	5	4	3	2	1

N	O	P	Q	R	S	T	U	V	W	X	Y	Z
26	25	24	23	22	21	20	19	18	17	16	15	14

"Oh!" said Hally. "That means A is now *13,* and Z equals *14!*"

"And he puts in periods to show where one number starts and ends, same as last time," Jason said.

"So what does it say?" Joe Kerry called through the screen door. He entered the kitchen, leaving Sam whining out on the deck.

"Haven't decoded it yet," Jason said. "I just cracked it."

"Well, hurry up. Eddie wants us to meet him down at the fire station. He says he's figured out a boat for us."

With the three older kids leaning over his shoulders, Jason smoothed the black code out flat on the table. He began to print in the letters that corresponded to each number written in silver ink.

13.26.10.21.25. 1 .9.20. 5 . 1 .9.21.5.18.9.9.20
A N D S O M E T I M E S I V E E T
.20.6.9. 1
T H E M

"'And…sometimes…I've…et'? 'I've et…them,'" he muttered as he printed.

"So if we add this to the three codes you've already received, we've got a poem!" Hally said, as she remembered the previous coded messages.

"Yeah," grunted Jason. "'Things that go bump in the night,'" he recited. "'Well, they never give me a fright. As for snakes, well, I've met 'em'…"

"'And sometimes I've et them'!" everyone chanted, repeating the last line together. They stared at each other.

"That's what happened to the rest of the rattlesnake!" Tuyet whispered. "He *ate* it!"

"A tough customer, whoever he is!" Joe muttered, nodding.

"And a rotten poet," Jason added. He was trying to look cool and unworried, Hally could tell, but his eyes were too wide.

"Well," she said, rumpling his hair, then grinning when he ducked and scowled at her, "guess we'll have to figure out what the masked rider means later on. But right now, Eddie's waiting for us."

When the Casecrackers reached the fire station where Eddie's father was chief, they found Eddie hard at work. On one side of the driveway, he was coiling a fire hose into an enormous spiral. "'Bout time you got here! I had to patch the whole thing by myself."

"Your dad's letting us have this?" Joe knelt to inspect the hose.

"Yup," Eddie grunted without stopping. "It got burned pretty bad in a fire last week. I patched the burned spots, but the crew'll never be able to use it again. Hydrant water pressure is so strong, it'd just blow the patches off." He stood for a moment and stretched. "We have to give Dad back the end fittings when we're done, though. They're bronze and worth a lot. But we can use 'em for now. And they even loaned us screw-on caps, so everything's airtight."

"This is supposed to be a boat?" Jason snorted.

"Will be when we're done, shrimp." Eddie continued coiling. "Hally, you and Joe take that string. Tuyet, you take this one. Start tying the coils to each other, so it'll stay coiled up. Like a big braided rug."

"What can I do?" Jason asked.

"You can stay out of trouble," Eddie said, "if that's possible."

"Watch Sam for me," Joe suggested. "I don't want him straying into the street."

Hally smiled to herself. Sam had already flopped onto his side on the sun-warmed concrete, and was starting to snore. Jason was more likely to stray than he was.

But Jason stayed to watch and toss insults while they tied the last of the coils together. "Won't float," he predicted.

"Wait and see." Eddie hurried off, then returned with a small engine on a wheeled cart. "Portable air compressor," he explained. "Dad will loan it to us on race day." He hooked up a hose from the compressor to one end of the fire hose.

"You've got to be kidding!" jeered someone from behind them.

The Casecrackers turned to find that three boys had halted their bicycles nearby. Standing astride a racing bike, B. Stuyvesant Van Zandt IV surveyed their efforts with an arrogant smirk. "If it floats at all, that thing'll be fast as a jellyfish! We'll all die of boredom, waiting for you to cross the finish line."

"Don't be so sure," Eddie growled. He yanked

on a cord like a lawnmower's cord. The compressor started with a roar. The flattened hose
began to swell and grow round. The bulge of air
crept along the hose, spiraling inward toward
the center of the coil.

"It's working!" Tuyet cried.

"And what did you pay for that hose?" Stuyvesant called.

Eddie glared at him. "None of your business."

"Oh?" Stuyvesant's smile widened. "A fire
hose is city property, isn't it? And my father pays
city taxes. I'd say it *is* my business."

Joe strolled over to stand shoulder-to-shoulder
with Eddie. "The hose was a throwaway, Stuyvesant. We'll be happy to prove it."

"Or we could just stuff it down your throat,"
Jason offered.

Stuyvesant glared, then threw back his head
and whooped. "You and what army, squirt?"

"No, you don't!" said Hally, as Jason started
forward. She grabbed the back of his T-shirt.

"Don't you have anything better to do?" she added, glaring at Stuyvesant.

The boy next to Stuyvesant leaned over and said something in his ear, and the two of them snickered.

"*That* does it!" said Eddie, clenching his fists.

"Oh, look!" Tuyet shrieked.

Everyone turned. While they'd bickered, the hose had gone on inflating. Now the coil stood up from the concrete, swollen and rock hard. Even as they gaped, the sound of the compressor changed, like a car's engine downshifting on a hill.

"Look out!" Joe warned, just as the first string snapped. Another snapped—then another, as the hose began to straighten, bit by bit.

"Turn it off!" Eddie cried. He raced for the compressor, with Jason scampering ahead of him. Eddie swerved to avoid him, but tripped over Sam. All three collapsed in a tangle.

The center end of the hose broke free and

reared like an angry snake. More strings popped. Stuyvesant was hooting so hard that he fell off his bicycle. On the street, traffic halted while drivers gaped.

The hose reared higher, and Joe tackled it. "Help!" he yelled, trying to wrestle it back to the ground. The hose shook him off and whipped out across the parking lot. Giggling wildly, Tuyet skittered backward out of its way. She tripped and sat down hard.

Hally knelt by the compressor and looked at it frantically. There had to be an off button here somewhere!

"No!" Jason howled.

Hally turned to see half a dozen firefighters, led by Eddie's father, storming out of the station. Three of them brandished fire axes!

"Don't kill it!" Jason pleaded, but it was too late. One axe blade after another chopped into the hose.

Like a great dying snake, the fire hose sagged,

drooped its bronze head, then went limp. Slowly, it began to flatten.

A fireman leaned past Hally to press a button, and the compressor's racket stopped. Clutching their ribs, Stuyvesant and his friends were groaning with glee. Out on the street, car horns honked congratulations. Several drivers cheered, then drove on.

"*Not* a good idea," Chief Machado said sternly, swinging his glare to include all the Casecrackers. But his lips twitched.

"Yes, sir," Eddie mumbled, getting to his feet. "Clean this mess up," the chief directed. "Hose goes in the dumpster, and bring me the end fittings." He and his crew stalked back into the station, with axes swinging and their shoulders shaking with silent laughter.

"Thanks for the show!" Stuyvesant chortled while his friends collected their bikes. "You still planning to beat me, townie girl?"

Hally didn't bother to look up. "Bet on it,

you snob," she muttered as the Casecrackers grimly turned their backs and set to work. "You can count on it."

"Then see ya at the races!" Stuyvesant jeered, and he rode away.

CHAPTER
4

GOTCHA!

"Why does Tuyet want to meet us at the library?" Eddie grumbled as he hurried down Spring Street with Hally and Jason. It was the next day, and he was still smarting from the fire-hose disaster.

"She's been helping Uncle Chau-Li at the restaurant," Hally said. "She called me from there. She has an idea for the mast for our boat, but she wants to show you a picture—if she can find one in a book."

"And I'm going to get a book on snakes," Jason said. "Maybe if we know what kind of rattler that rattle came from...That'll give us a clue to who's sending my codes." The trio cut across the grass and uphill toward the library, which sat in the middle of a big, green park. "There's Joe and Tuyet," Jason added. "And Sam."

"What's got into them?" Eddie wondered.

Joe was waving his arms at them, and Tuyet was bouncing up and down. Sam pranced and swung his tail. "Come see!" Tuyet grabbed Hally by the arm and towed her toward a bike rack. "It's the masked rider's bike!" She touched the shiny black fender of a mountain bike that was chained there.

"You're sure?" Hally asked.

"Positive!" Joe tapped the playing card that was laminated and mounted on a piece of stiff plastic, then bolted to the back fender like a license plate. "What did I tell you? The Ace of Hearts!"

"What do you think that means?" Eddie asked. No one had a clue.

"So where is he?" Jason swung around, as if

the masked rider might leap out from behind one of the big elms that shaded the park.

"In the library?" Tuyet guessed.

"Or downtown," Hally said. The library was only a block from the waterfront, where many of the town's businesses were located.

"Wherever he is, we've got a problem," Eddie said. "How do we catch him if we don't know what he looks like?"

"Unless he's wearing his mask," Jason said hopefully.

The older kids laughed. "Not likely he'll do that here!" Joe said. "People might stare."

Jason looked huffy. "So what? A guy who eats rattlesnakes is gonna care if people think he's weird? They would anyway."

"How about this?" Hally suggested. "If we watch from inside the library lobby, we can see the bike rack. Then, wherever the rider comes from, we'll see him when he goes to unlock his bike."

"Right!" Eddie cried. "Then we dash out and nab him!"

The Casecrackers hustled up the long ramp to the library, then filed in through its outer doors. Between the outer doors of tinted glass and the inner doors, also of glass, was a small lobby with a display case and a bulletin board. "No place to sit," Eddie complained.

"But the view's perfect." Hally put her nose to the outer glass.

"Do you think he'll be long?" Jason wondered. Waiting wasn't one of his talents.

"Uh oh," Joe said, slapping his forehead. "Wait a minute. What if he spots us here? He knows what *we* look like, even if we don't know him. He might just leave his bike and walk away."

"I know what we can do." Tuyet grabbed Jason and tugged him toward the inner doors. "We'll be back in a minute."

While they waited, Eddie, Hally, and Joe watched the bike. Each time someone exited the library, they casually turned their backs to study the display case. "Think that's him?" Eddie whispered, as a man left the lobby with his arms full of books.

"Too short," Joe said. "And too flabby. The rider's in shape. I bet he rides that bike a lot." They watched as the man crossed the parking lot to a car and unlocked the door. "See?"

"Here," said Tuyet as she joined them. She and Jason held half a dozen books. "We can think about boats and hide at the same time. When somebody comes, hold one of these in front of your face."

It was hard not to laugh, but Tuyet's plan seemed to work. Each time someone left the library, up went five books in front of five faces. As the person headed down the ramp, the Casecrackers would slowly lower their books and peek after the suspect.

"That guy's really staring back at us!" Eddie chortled.

"Not the rider, though," Hally giggled. The man went to a car.

"Ooops, here comes somebody!" Jason hissed. Everyone yanked a book up.

"May I help you children?" asked a woman, her stern voice not sounding at all helpful.

Hally lowered her book and found Mrs. Pibbitt, the one librarian at the Newport Library who never smiled, not smiling at them. Her skinny eyebrows were raised.

"You could help *him.*" Joe jerked his thumb at Jason.

"Huh?" Jason glanced from Joe to the librarian. "Oh yeah! Yeah, I need to look up something, and I don't know how to use the computer." He gave her a brave, pitiful smile.

Mrs. Pibbitt's nose twitched, as if she could smell a fib. Jason kept on smiling. "Very well," she sniffed at last. "Come along."

As Jason followed her into the library, he turned back to make a face at the Casecrackers.

"Can't use a computer, my eye!" muttered Hally, after the door closed behind Jason. "He knows more about Dad's computer than Dad does."

"And he thinks on his feet," Joe admitted.

"Here!" said Tuyet, holding her book where they all could see. "This is the way we should make our boat sail. With a...," she read the caption under a picture of a boat, "With a junk rig. I remember these from Vietnam."

"Weird kind of rig," Eddie said, studying the picture.

"We could make the crosspieces, these things, from bamboo," Tuyet said, her eyes shining. "My uncle Chau-Li has many bamboo fishing poles in the basement that we could borrow."

"I've got a blue plastic tarp. Should do for the sail," Joe said.

"I bet we'll be the only junk rig in the crazy race," Eddie said. "But we still need a hull—the part of the boat we ride in."

Glancing up from the book, Hally realized that several people had left the library, and that a tall black man stood across the lobby, reading the bulletin board. "Shhh!" Hally warned the others.

The man gave a bored shrug and departed whistling, without looking their way. They watched him and the others stroll down the ramp. None of them went near the bike rack. Jason shoved open the inner door. "Thanks a whole heap, Joe!"

Joe laughed. "It was all I could think of. Where is she now?"

"I got her to help me look up 'bout a jillion articles on pygmy rattlers. She's down in the basement getting the magazines."

The outer door opened. A boy in a white uniform stood there, holding a pizza box. "Are you guys the Kerry Hill Casecrackers?"

"Yes," Hally said, "but—"

"Then this is for you," he said, handing her

the box. "And here's your drinks." He handed a bag to Tuyet, then he headed out the door. As he left, he almost bumped a young woman in a blue uniform.

"Kerry Hill Casecrackers?"

"Yes!" Eddie said blissfully, reaching for the white box she held.

"Wait a minute!" Joe objected, but she was gone already.

"Wow!" Eddie put his nose to the box and inhaled. "Pepperoni!"

"Kerry Hill Casecrackers?" asked two voices at once. Two more pizza delivery boys pushed into the lobby.

"Yes," Hally said helplessly, "but we didn't—"

But Eddie was already taking their boxes to stack on top of his first.

"Just *what* is going on out here?" Her arms full of magazines, Mrs. Pibbitt stood glaring from the inner doorway. Her outraged eyes took in Eddie's pizzas, then swung to a delivery girl who was marching up the ramp with a pizza box held high. "You can't eat in the library!" she declared. "How dare you even *think* of bringing pizza into the library!"

"Pizza for the Kerry Hill Casecrackers!" the girl announced, as she entered the lobby. "That you guys?"

"*Out!*" thundered Mrs. Pibbit, pointing the way. The magazines slipped from her grip and hit the floor. "Out, all of you!" A group of people trying to leave the library edged past her. One man stooped to pick up the magazines. He handed them to her, then hurried away.

"But who gets the nine-inch pizza?" the delivery girl asked.

"We do!" Eddie said, grabbing it, "and, yes ma'am, we're getting out. Right this minute."

"And don't try sneaking back!" cried Mrs. Pibbitt. She practically shoved them and the delivery girl out the doors, then stood scowling at them through the glass.

"What an old crab!" said the girl. She trotted off down the ramp.

"We'd better try to explain," said Hally.

"Or apologize," agreed Tuyet.

"But the pizza will get cold," Eddie objected.

"And Mrs. Pibbitt doesn't want to hear it right now," added Joe. "Besides, what I want to know is..." He turned to look toward the bike rack.

The others followed his gaze, and they all let out a collective groan. "The bike!" cried Tuyet.

"That sneak!" said Hally. The bike with the ace license plate was gone!

Joe laughed. "Smart guy! So that's what was going on!"

"It was all a diversion," Hally agreed. "He must have spotted us. So he ordered pizzas—probably paid for them over the phone with a credit card."

"If he spotted us, he didn't see us from outside," Jason said. "'Cause the glass is too dark."

"That means he walked right by us!" Tuyet said. "He must have phoned from inside. Then

57

he had to walk by us to get to his bike."

But lots of people had passed them in the last half hour. There was no saying which one had been the rider.

"Meantime, our pizza's getting cold," Eddie pointed out. "Let's have a picnic over there, under that tree."

The final mystery of the day came when they opened the third box, which held a nine-inch sausage and green pepper pizza. "Look at those numbers!" cried Hally, as Eddie lifted the lid.

On the inside of the box, someone had printed a series of numbers and dots. "It looks like the last code!"

12.9.20.20.9.22. 2.19.11.3. 26.9.16.20 20.5.1.9,
11.13.21.9.11.22.13.11.3.9.22.21!
13.11.9

"Lemme see!" Jason took the box. He stared at it, then pulled a stub of pencil from his pocket. Printing out a key to the last code, he sat frowning at it, his lips moving. Then he fell back in the grass and laughed, the pizza balanced on his stomach. "He got us!"

"What's it say!" they demanded. "What's it say?"

"It says 'Better luck next time, Casecrackers!' And he signed it—'Ace!'"

5

RUNAWAY ICE CUBE

"Why the ice house?" Hally called. Twelve feet ahead, Tuyet walked with the front half of a bundle of bamboo poles balanced on her shoulder. Hally carried the back half. Jason kept running back and forth under the poles, getting in their way.

"Joe wouldn't say," Tuyet called back. "Just said to meet him there at 2:00, and that he'd tell Eddie."

The Casecrackers hadn't met as a group for two days. Joe had worked yesterday as a tour guide at the Maitland Manor, the big Bellevue Avenue mansion-museum where his father was curator. And Eddie had gone out fishing for bluefish with his cousin.

Left to their own devices, Hally and Tuyet had ransacked Tuyet's basement. Using the bamboo poles and rope they found, they'd built a junk rig. Joe had asked Tuyet to bring it today. He would supply the hull and a tarp for the sail, he'd promised.

The ice house was built out on one of the harbor wharves. At one time, it had supplied ice to the fishing fleet to keep the catch cold at sea. Nowadays it supplied block ice to yachts and restaurants. Joe stood beyond it on a bulkhead, looking down at the water. He turned and waved. "Great," he said, coming to meet them. "We're all here." He pointed a thumb over his shoulder. "Eddie's down there in his dinghy with Sam. *Netop* is our chase boat for the test run."

"So where's *your* boat?" demanded Jason.

"Coming right up." Joe put two fingers to his mouth, and let out an ear-splitting whistle.

A man standing next to the ice house gave him a thumbs-up, then hit a button in the wall. A garage door rose. The man disappeared, and a moment later, a pickup backed into view.

The truck stopped beside them, and Joe opened its tailgate. Everyone gasped. A solid block of ice—as big as the truck bed, and a good foot and a half thick—sat there!

"A giant ice cube!" Hally touched it. "For a boat?"

Joe laughed. "Why not? Ice floats. And the race is only a half a mile long. It shouldn't melt before we cross the finish line. I asked my friend Mike here to freeze it in his truck, so we could move it."

"Coooooool," Jason crooned, then laughed at his pun.

"Let's rig it first," called Eddie, rising into view as he climbed the ladder that was nailed to the bulkhead. "It'll be easier than in the water."

Working quickly in the summer heat, the Casecrackers spread out Tuyet's junk rig on the ground. The girls had lashed the five longest bamboo poles together to make one thick mast. Then they had tied four shorter poles crosswise to the mast at two-foot intervals. The poles could be folded to carry, or fanned out to make the rig. With it fanned out, the friends tied the blue tarp to the crosspieces, which would keep the sail spread to the wind.

"But how do we make the rig stand up on the ice?" Jason asked.

"Easy!" said Joe. "I cast a length of pipe into the ice for a mast step. We drop the butt of the mast into the pipe. Then, to keep the rig standing, we've cast a hook made of steel bar into each corner of the ice. See?" He tapped a loop of rusty metal sticking up from a corner of the cube. "We just tie four ropes—the stays— from the top of the mast to each hook."

In less than ten minutes, the junk rig was in

place. "Let's launch this sucker quick," Eddie fretted, "before she melts."

With the truck backed to the edge of the bulkhead, Joe and Mike climbed up on its sides. The truck bed had been lined with a wide sheet of plastic before the cube was frozen. This slippery lining allowed the ice to slide. Mike and Joe edged the cube backward.

While Mike and Joe were moving the truck in place, Eddie had rowed his dinghy far out from the bulkhead. Sam stood in its stern, wagging his tail and whining. "It's gonna make a monster splash," Eddie warned. "Everybody stand back!"

The slab slid, tilted, and dropped! Water splashed to the sky, and the junk rig wobbled wildly. But it didn't topple. Everyone ran back to the edge of the bulkhead and cheered. "It floats!" cried Hally.

"Told you." Holding a rope that he'd tied to one hook in the ice cube, Joe started down the ladder. "So let's see how she sails."

Hally, Jason, and Joe took the ice boat. Eddie, Tuyet, and Sam followed in the dinghy, with Eddie shouting directions. "Pull the starboard— the right side, Hally—of the sail toward the back of the boat and keep it there. We're lucky the wind's from the south, or we'd never get her out past the piers."

"My bottom's wet," Jason complained. They'd made him sit down, since the ice was slippery. "And it's cold!"

"Rudder more to port, Joe," Eddie commanded. They'd fashioned a steering rudder from an old oar, which was tied to the stern of the cube, midway between the two back hooks.

"We're gonna ram that ship," Jason warned. An enormous, glossy yacht flying a British flag was tied along the end of the pier, and the cube was edging closer and closer. To Hally it seemed they were drifting sideways almost as fast as they were going forward!

A crewman in starched white leaned over the yacht's varnished rail. "Keep that...that... *thing* off my topsides!"

In the end, Eddie threw them a towline and towed the cube out past the end of the docks. Then he set them loose again, out in the channel. "Head downwind," he called. "That'll be easier. Hally, let your right corner loose so the sail lies square across the cube."

With the wind behind them, the cube began to pick up speed. "It's working!" Tuyet cried. Sam barked his approval.

"All *right!*" Jason crowed. "We're beating Eddie and Tuyet. Come on, you slowpokes!"

A motor launch carrying sailors in from the moorings roared past at a distance. Passengers pointed and waved.

"Look, there's Dad!" Far across the harbor, Hally could see a fleet of tiny white sails. It was the children's class that her father taught in his summer job as an instructor for the Newport

66

Sailing Club. She could see his small motorboat circling the stragglers in his fleet, like a collie herding stray sheep. "Think he'll see us?"

Joe laughed. "We're not sitting three inches out of the water. He might spot our sail, but I doubt it."

"Yo!" Eddie yelled from his dinghy.

Everyone turned to look. A dark blue sailboat was coming up fast from the rear. Eddie jerked a thumb at it and made a face.

"Oh, no!" said Hally, "Is that—"

It was. The sailboat swept past them. Holding his varnished tiller, Stuyvesant the Snob shot them a look of disbelief. The two boys sailing with him pointed and jeered.

"Jerks!" said Joe. "Just ignore them."

"Good luck!" Hally muttered, as the sailboat cut across their course, then turned again. "With him sailing circles around us?"

"You gotta be kidding!" Stuyvesant hooted, as he tacked his boat and nearly clipped their stern. "That's not a junk rig, it's a piece of junk!"

His bow wave slopped against the ice and splashed aboard just as Joe turned to glare. He skidded on the wet ice and sat down hard. The cube tilted with his weight, and Joe slid into the harbor, his face the picture of astonishment!

Stuyvesant and his friends howled with delight.

"Oh, gosh!" said Hally, looking behind. Eddie had stopped to collect Joe. Tuyet was trying to haul him into the dinghy, with too much help from Sam.

Meanwhile, Hally had her own problems. "Here, Jase!" Hally handed over the two ropes that controlled the bottom edges of the sail. She grabbed the tiller. "Uh oh!" she said, looking ahead. The cube was fast approaching the north corner of the harbor. If they kept sailing straight, they'd plow right into the floats at the Newport Yacht Club!

"Turn it!" Jason yelled. "You gotta turn!"

In the distance, Eddie was screaming at them.

"Push your tiller to..." Hally couldn't hear the rest of his words. But they needed to sail to the left, just as they'd needed to go left back at the pier. She shoved the oar to the right, as Joe had done. "Pull in the right corner of the sail, Jase. *Hurry!*"

Jason pulled, but the wind-filled sail was too big for him. Hauling hard on the rope, he leaned back, gave a grunt of effort—and his feet flew out from under him! Hally watched in open-mouthed horror as he slid bottomfirst off the ice!

"Got him!" Eddie yelled, rowing desperately. The blue boat skimmed up alongside Hally. Stuyvesant was laughing so hard that one of his friends had taken over steering. "I love it!" Stuyvesant whooped. "Townie girl on a runaway ice cube!"

Hally gave him a ferocious scowl. His boat jibed away and she looked ahead. Fifty feet in front of her, at the yacht club docks, the club launch sat idling, waiting for passengers. Its driver looked up from a book. His jaw dropped. He leaned frantically over the boat's side, yanked at docking lines, straightened, and rammed an engine control forward. The launch shot out of the way like a spat watermelon seed—and Hally's ice boat bombed the dock!

6

MAYBE IT'S A TRAP

"You're sure you're not hurt?" Tuyet asked again, as they dropped the battered junk rig in Hally's backyard.

"All that's hurt is my pride," Hally insisted. At least, that was what hurt the worst. Her bruises would fade, and the splinters from her collision with the dock planking could be dug out. It was the launch driver's lecture and Stuyvesant the Snob's laughter that still stung.

"You ain't gonna believe this!" Jason called, returning from the mailbox. "It's another code! But this one came by mail—it's got a postmark. And it's written in black ink on white paper, instead of silver on black like the others."

"Same code or a harder one this time?" Hally asked.

"Same one," said Jason, reading the code as they climbed the stairs to the deck. "Hang on a minute, and I'll tell you what it says."

"Change your clothes first, before you drip all over everything." Joe had gone home with Eddie to borrow dry clothes. Then they were coming over for a Casecracker council of war. Ice cubes were out, everyone had grimly agreed. But they needed a boat design, and they needed it fast. They had only three days left until the crazy race.

Ten minutes later, splinter-free and dry, Hally joined the others at the picnic table on the deck. Jason had set out bread with peanut butter, bananas, pickle relish and honey for sandwiches. Everyone was making a sandwich—everybody but Jason without relish—while Jason broke the code. At last he frowned, set down his pencil, and turned it so the others could read.

"'In the basement. 1012 Bellevue,'" Hally read. "'Ace.'"

"*What's* in the basement?" wondered Eddie.

"Or *who*?" Tuyet made a face. "Ugh! I don't like basements anyway. And to meet a man with a mask in one?"

"There's five of us to one of him," Joe pointed out. "And Sam."

"Great!" Hally laughed. "Sam'll lick him to death."

"Or bash him with his tail, like he does me," Jason agreed. "Still, even if it's a trap, we gotta go look. How else are we gonna crack this case?"

Nobody had an answer to that.

"What bothers me," Hally said later, as they trooped down Bellevue Avenue, "is why did the pattern change? Why'd this code come on a Wednesday, instead of a Friday or a Monday like it usually does?" They were walking past some of Newport's famous castle-like "summer cottages," which had been built by the very rich in the last century.

"And why'd he mail it instead of deliver it?" added Joe.

"And why the color change—black ink on white paper this time?" Tuyet wondered.

Jason shrugged. "Maybe he ran out of silver ink?"

"Or somebody else sent you this code!" Hally stopped short as it hit her.

"We've got *two* mysterious code senders instead of one?" Joe frowned and shook his head. "One's weird enough, Hally."

"It would explain the change in style."

"You think whoever sent this code is somebody else, pretending to be Ace?" Joe scoffed. "And this new guy wants to meet us in a basement?"

"Maybe we better trade Sam in on a Doberman!" Eddie sounded as if he was only half teasing.

One thousand twelve Bellevue turned out to be a mansion, not far from Joe's own home at Maitland Manor. "It was turned into condos years ago," he told them as they stared up at its dark, ivy-covered walls. "I guess maybe two dozen people live here."

"Could this be Ace's home?" Tuyet wondered aloud.

If it was, he wasn't listed by that name, the Casecrackers discovered when they checked the nameplates on the mailboxes inside the huge front hall. "Don't recognize anybody," Joe admitted.

"And we can't get to the basement through here," reported Eddie, who'd been trying all the doors that led off the hall. "It's locked tight as a drum."

But that wasn't the case when they circled the mansion outside. In the back, a stone stairway led down to a door set at basement level. The door stood ajar.

"It's like someone's waiting," Tuyet whispered. "I don't like this!"

Neither did anyone else, Hally could tell. And they liked it less when they found that the light switch inside the door didn't work.

"Bulb's burned out," Joe said, as he flicked the switch up and down.

"Or he took the bulb!" Jason suggested with ghoulish pleasure.

"Sam goes in first." Joe shoved the big retriever into the darkness. "He'll tell us if somebody's in there."

But Sam merely drooped his ears and skulked back to the door. He stood gazing up at his owner, his tail waving.

"Does that mean 'yeah, he's in there, boss, but he's too big to deal with'?" Eddie laughed. "Or 'gee, I dunno, I'm just a dog'?" He dug a book of matches out of his pocket. "Come on, you guys, let's do it."

Holding hands, they followed Eddie into the

dark. After a dozen steps, he stopped to strike a match. In the match's brief glow, Hally's eyes darted wildly around. That big, hulking shape in the middle of the room was a furnace. She made out a lawnmower, some tools—

The light went out.

"Nothing here." Jason sounded disappointed.

Eddie's hand tugged them on. "Watch it, there's a doorway here— Yuk!" He ducked backward and bumped into Hally.

"What is it?"

Eddie made a spitting sound. *"Phhh!* Cobweb!" He took a deep breath, then towed them on.

In the second room, then the third, the light from Eddie's matches showed them nothing but junk—old bicycles, trunks, snow tires, and other things Hally couldn't identify in the gloom.

In the room after that, something brushed her face. "Ugh!" She batted the thing away. It touched her again! "Ick! It's after me!" She dodged backward, breaking their chain. Everyone shrieked and bumped each other. Things fell and clattered.

A match flared, then Eddie burst out laughing. In the center of the room, a string with a tiny pull swayed to and fro. "There's your critter!" He pulled it, and light flooded the room.

Squinting in the welcome brightness, they giggled with relief, then—

"Look!" Tuyet pointed.

Against the far wall stood a jumble of wooden shapes, like pieces of broken furniture. A white paper was pinned to the pile.

"A note?" Joe started toward it.

"In code!" said Jason, who reached it first. "And—*Yow!* Look how he stuck it here!"

The code was pinned to one piece of wood with an icepick.

15.25.19.22.21, 5.8. 15.25.19.
11.13.26. 19.21.9. 5.20.
13.11.9

"Let's get out of here!" Tuyet groaned.

"Not till we read this!" protested Jason. "Gimme a minute, I've practically got this code memorized."

While he translated the message, the other Casecrackers turned outward, to face the shadows, and stood shoulder to shoulder. Hally could feel her heart thump-thumping in her chest. She kept her eyes on Sam's ears. Surely he'd prick them if anyone crept near?

But Sam's ears still dangled at ease when Jason said, "Got it!" He laughed under his breath. "It says this is for us if we want it. From Ace."

"But what is it?" Tuyet wondered.

Joe stooped to look. "It's a bed frame. An old four-poster. See, these are the side boards, and here's the headboard."

Jason snorted. "Why'd Ace think we want an old bed? He thinks we've got nothing better to do than haul his junk to the junkyard for him?"

"Ho!" Hally clapped her hands and spun in

a circle. "I don't know why Ace is giving us his bed, but you know what we can do with it?" She patted it and laughed aloud. "Casecrackers, you are looking at our next yacht. And we'll call it the...Snoozer Cruiser!"

CHAPTER
7

THE SNOOZER CRUISER

"You've got everything you need to build this battleship?" Jim Watkins asked. Hally and Jason's father glanced in the rearview mirror of the pickup truck. The four-poster bed rode in the back, along with Joe, Sam, Tuyet, and Eddie. The junk rig was also stowed there, along with lots of large plastic buckets, string, and odds and ends.

"I think so," said Hally, looking back and making a face at Joe.

"Shift to third now," Mr. Watkins said as he stepped on the clutch.

Scowling with fierce concentration, Jason

moved the truck's gearshift from second gear to third.

"Nice," said his father. "That's just right." Jason patted out a little drumbeat of proud excitement on his own knees.

The truck belonged to Joe's cousin Frank. Its name was "the Baitmobile," and Frank used it only for carrying his smelly bait and lobstering gear around town.

He'd driven past the Casecrackers yesterday, while they were straggling home with the bedstead, and had given them a ride. Then when he heard what they were up to, he offered them his truck till Sunday. The bedstead was too big to fit easily into the Watkins's car, anyway. And Frank was off to visit his girlfriend in Boston, traveling in what he called his courting car.

Right now the Baitmobile was bound for King's Park, on the south side of the harbor. The little park beach would be the site of the crazy race the day after tomorrow. So it would be the best place to build the Snoozer Cruiser and test-sail her, Eddie had decreed.

"Back to second gear..." Mr. Watkins directed, *"Now."*

This time, Jason clashed the gears. The Baitmobile screeched like a wounded bobcat, but their father didn't say a thing. He just ruffled Jason's hair. Jason sat back, disgusted.

"How goes the case of the mysterious codes?" Mr. Watkins asked.

"We might crack it tomorrow." Hally started to tell him about their plan, but they'd arrived at King's Park. The truck bounced down a slope to the tiny crescent of beach, and wheezed to a stop. The other Casecrackers tumbled out of the back and began unloading.

"I'll pick you up at four," said Mr. Watkins, looking at his watch. "I've got an hour between my juniors racing class and my evening adult class. So be here and be ready to go. And Eddie, if she sails well, sail over near the fort. I'll be looking out for you guys." He tugged Hally's braid, gave Jason a mock punch on his shoulder, and was soon driving off to work.

"Tide's coming in," Eddie said with satisfaction. "So I say we build her right at the edge of the water. She'll be almost afloat by the time we've got her put together."

They'd worked out the plans the night before, then everyone had scattered to collect the parts. Tuyet had scored the eight-gallon plastic buckets from the restaurant where her uncle Chau-Li worked.

Eddie brought miles of rope and string, and some duct tape.

Joe scrounged half a sheet of plywood and some two-by-fours. With these and his father's power tools, he'd built what he called a barn-door rudder. They'd use it to steer their boat.

Hally had persuaded Mr. Ames, the owner of the Watkins's apartment, to part with some screws and a full sheet of plywood. At five dollars, it was their only expense so far.

Jason had brought something too, but he wasn't saying what, except that they'd all be astounded and envious. His contribution was hidden in a rolled paper bag that he guarded jealously.

Eddie studied the harbor water lapping at his bare feet, then his old battered diver's watch. "We only have two hours on race day to build her, so let's time this, okay? Ready...*set*..."

They began. Tuyet and Jason clapped lids on buckets, then taped them to make sure they would be waterproof. The others assembled the bed. Its side boards had flat metal hooks that dropped into slots in the headboard and footboard to lock the four parts together.

Once that was done, they tied the buckets in place. Beneath the mattress—if the bed had had a mattress—the buckets lay on their sides in rows, four across by three long. "Like pontoons," said Joe. "They'll be great flotation."

When they'd secured the buckets in a web of ropes, they topped them with the sheet of plywood. "Makes a nice sturdy deck," said Eddie. Using a hand drill, he bored holes all around its edges. Hally and Tuyet followed him, screwing the deck to the bedframe.

Meanwhile, Joe attached a metal bracket to the outer face of the footboard. His rudder already had a matching bracket screwed onto its rudder post. "We'll drop the rudder into place after we push out into deep water," he explained as he finished. "'Cause the rudder'll hang a bit below the bed legs for good steerage."

"One hour," warned Eddie, checking his watch.

Using some scrap metal strapping, Eddie and Hally constructed two loops that he bolted to the midpoint and base of the headboard. "To hold the mast butt," he said.

Once that was done, they dropped the junk rig in place. The stays were tied from the top of the mast to the two back bedposts.

"And that's it!" Joe stood back to admire their work.

"Not quite," said Jason. "Every boat needs a figurehead."

The Casecrackers looked at the object he pulled from his bag and burst out laughing. It was a green, snaggle-toothed, hook-nosed Halloween mask with frizzy red hair, stuffed with socks to hold its shape.

"Perfect!" chortled Eddie. "When Stuyvesant sees us coming, he'll quake in his shiny white, polished yachting sneakers. Let's nail her and sail her." He nailed the mask to the front of the headboard, so that it glared out over the incoming tide.

Strapping on their life jackets, they surrounded the Snoozer Cruiser and half-lifted, half-shoved her out to sea. "Climb aboard," Eddie commanded as the junk sail started to fill. "We're underway."

Quickly Joe dropped his rudder into its bracket. Eddie took the tiller—the length of two-by-four which turned the rudder—and off they sailed. "She moves," Eddie said, as they floated past the first line of moorings. "This is where the starting line will be, and the course goes thataway, out to the channel."

He swung the tiller, and the Cruiser slipped past a lobster pot. "Handles really well!" Joe noted.

From her seat on the deck, Hally could see the distant, gleaming walls of the yacht club. She brushed the hair out of her eyes, then shook a fist toward the island. "Look out, B. Stuyvesant Van Zandt, you snob," she yelled at the distant docks. "We're coming to get you!"

"So she goes downwind," said Joe, "but will she reach?"

Eddie shrugged. "Bring in the starboard sheet, Tuyet."

"Speak English!" she teased.

"That line you're holding." Eddie nodded at her rope, which was tied to the bottom edge of the sail, "It's called a sheet. And it's the sheet on the right, or starboard, side of the boat, Tuyet, so it's the starboard sheet. Now would you pull on the thing, so we can turn?"

"Aye-aye, Captain!" Tuyet hauled the sheet in. Eddie swung the tiller, and the Cruiser moved slowly but surely to the left. *Port,* Hally reminded herself.

"We've got us a *boat!*" Joe whooped. He slapped a low five with Eddie, then a high five with Hally, who passed it on to Tuyet. Jason brought it around full circle and back to Joe, then they all cheered.

"There's Dad's class!" Jason yelled, pointing toward the fort. "Can we go show him?"

Eddie shook his head. "They're heading up into Brenton Cove, Jase, dead upwind, and with a head start. We'd never catch 'em."

"But there's Dad, and I think he sees us!"

Hally said, as a boat slid out from behind the flock of sails. "Is he looking this way?"

The distant figure stood in the boat, and raised something overhead. A second later, they heard his salute—the *Hoooooonk-Honk-Honk!* of a freon-powered foghorn. Everyone waved.

"Let's jibe and run down by Goat Island," Eddie suggested.

Under his orders, Tuyet eased the starboard sheet. After they'd turned downwind, Hally brought in the port sheet, and they angled to the right.

"Don't look now!" groaned Joe, pointing behind them.

Running down from the yacht club docks came a familiar blue sailboat. "Harden up, Hally!" said Eddie. "Pull your port sheet all the way in," he translated, when she made a face. "I don't want him seeing how fast we are till race day, so we'll change course."

But Stuyvesant also changed his course so

he could continue to pursue them.

"Oh well, we tried," Eddie said, shrugging his shoulders.

Joe shook his head. "That guy thinks everything in life's a contest. I bet he tries to set records when he washes the dishes."

Eddie snorted. "He never washed a dish in his life!"

The blue boat was gaining, but slowly. "We are *fast!*" Eddie crowed. "He'll catch us eventually, but he won't catch us on Saturday—not in any homemade boat. And I think he's starting to get the picture." As he spoke, the blue boat jibed away, and winged off toward Goat Island. "Yahhh!" Eddie yelled after him. "See ya on Saturday, Stuyvesant!"

But if the snob heard Eddie, he didn't turn to acknowledge him.

"So how about a sail around the harbor?" Eddie said. "We'll circle the main harbor, then back to the beach." They jibed again to head down the navigation channel, past the ends of all the long piers. People in fishing boats stopped working and laughed, and tourists stared from the docks. A big tour boat passed them port to port with a toot of its horn.

They were approaching the corner of the harbor, where Hally's runaway ice cube had failed to make its turn. "Starboard sheet comes in, Tuyet. Hally ease the port." The bed turned gracefully. Eddie grinned with pride, then, as he looked ahead in their new direction, his grin vanished.

Steaming toward them from Goat Island, with all its lights flashing like the lights of a police patrol car, came a large white powerboat with a red diagonal slash painted down its side!

"The Coast Guard cutter!" Joe groaned. "We're busted!"

"And guess who was the rat who ratted on us?" growled Eddie. He nodded beyond the oncoming vessel, where Stuyvesant's blue boat tacked, heading upwind for his yacht club.

A woman in blue uniform stepped out onto the cutter's foredeck and lifted a loud-hailer to her mouth. "We're coming alongside, Mr. Machado!"

"You know her?" Hally asked.

"Yeah, we're friends," Eddie muttered. "I'm friends with all the crew, but believe me, that won't cut us any slack out here."

Tuyet frowned. "Why would they bust us?"

"We've got life jackets, but there's a lot of required gear, like a fog horn, that we don't have aboard," Eddie explained grimly, as they slacked the sheets and stood by for the Coasties to board them. "The rules are relaxed for the crazy race. But today's not race day, and we're out in the main harbor."

"They're gonna arrest us?" Jason asked hopefully.

"No, but they could fine me if they feel like it. More likely, Captain McGonagle's gonna give us a lecture on proper seamanship and a rap on the knuckles." Eddie's face was very pink.

When the Coasties concluded that the Snoozer Cruiser wasn't properly equipped for sea and decided to tow it back to dry land, Eddie's embarrassment was complete. Handing the tiller to Joe, he flopped down on the deck. Teeth clenched and arms tightly crossed, he glared up at the sky while the cutter towed them slowly back to King's Park.

Eddie didn't look when they passed close by Stuyvesant's blue boat, with its waving, smirking skipper.

"We're gonna *get* that sneaking, ratting, spoil-sport!" he swore, when they finally cast off the Coasties' line and sailed the last few yards to shore. "We're gonna beat that rich stinker, if it's the last thing we do."

Everyone shook hands on that promise. "We're gonna beat him!"

CHAPTER 8

KIDNAPPED!

"What time is it?" Jason asked.

"Four minutes later than the last time you asked." Standing astride her bike, Hally swatted a mosquito that had landed on her knee.

"They're bad back here," Joe agreed, as he scratched a bite on his back.

It was Friday, one of the days that Ace the Masked Rider usually delivered his mysterious codes. The Casecrackers were lying in ambush, behind a dense hedge of lilacs just down the street from the Watkins's house. Everyone stood astride a bike, except for Jason, who had tired of that. He lay on his stomach under the hedge, where he had a clear view of the front porch.

The plan was to dash out of hiding while Ace was off his bike, dropping his latest code in the mailbox. They'd surround him so that he couldn't ride away, then they'd demand an explanantion. Why was he sending Jason codes? What did he want?

"It's almost three," Eddie grumbled. "He's not coming today."

"He'll come," Jason insisted. "I know he will." He squirmed over onto his back to peer through the bushes upside down. Spying a soft spot, Sam sauntered over and flopped beside him. He propped his chin on Jason's stomach. Jason tugged absently at his ears.

"Waiiiiitt," murmured Eddie, who looked out through another gap in the hedge. "Is that— Yeah! Here he comes!"

Hally's hands tightened on her handlebars. Jason rolled out from under the bushes and grabbed his bike. "We're gonna get him!"

"Easy," said Joe. "Easy does it. We don't want to scare him away. Tell us when, Ed."

"He's looking all around and up at your windows," Eddie muttered. "Suspects some sort of trap, I bet. He's not dumb. Okaaaaay, he's setting his bike down. Get ready...He's headed up your porch steps...Get set..."

"*Go!*" yelled Jason, jumping the gun. Standing up on his pedals, he charged across the grass toward the gap in the hedge. The others groaned with frustration and sprinted after him. So much for their silent ambush!

"Woof!" Sam let out a bark and dashed after Jason.

Boy and dog reached the gap in the hedge at the same instant, with Hally right behind, and Joe half a length behind her.

"Watch it, you stupid mutt!" screamed Jason, as the retriever shouldered past him. He tipped into the bushes and fell. His bike blocked the gap just as Hally arrived!

"Hey!" she yelped, wobbling into the bushes on the other side.

Joe tried to swerve between the fallen bikes. His bike bumped over Jason's wheel. Head over handlebars, he crashed through the hedge gap and out onto the sidewalk. Tuyet pedaled over to help him.

"You bozos!" yelled Eddie. With his way blocked, he beat his fists on his knees with frustration.

Untangling her bike from the lilacs, Hally shoved it out onto the street.

Down the way, Ace stood on the porch, his hands braced on his hips. He was dressed all in black again, from his trousers to his ski mask. He shook his head at them. Hally bet he was grinning beneath that mask. Then he leaped off the porch and grabbed his bike.

"Catch him!" Jason screamed, popping out of the hedge. Leaves stuck out of his tousled hair, and twigs clung to his clothing.

Hally swung astride her bike while Joe leaped aboard his. "Get him, Sam!" Joe yelled, as the masked rider pedaled away.

Hally stood up on her pedals and pumped. She was gaining speed, and so was Joe beside her. But the rider had a head start. Sam shot down the street after him, barking merrily.

"Get him!" Joe yelled again. Out on the street at last, Eddie pulled alongside Hally, then passed her, his face grim, his body tucked low over his handlebars, legs pumping furiously.

But fast as Eddie was, the masked rider was faster. The only one who could catch him was Sam. His tail waving, he raced alongside the speeding black mountain bike. Ace reached down to pat his head just as they reached the corner.

"*Sam!*" Joe cried, but he was too winded. His voice didn't carry. Sam shot around the corner after the bike and was gone.

"We'll never catch him!" Panting, Hally glided to a stop.

Tuyet drew up beside her. "He's too fast!"

Far down the block, Eddie and Joe rounded the corner. They vanished in pursuit of the rider.

"Maybe Sam will stop him." Jason sat down on the sidewalk to examine a scraped knee.

As much fun as he was having? Good luck! Hally just hoped Sam had sense enough to drop out of the race in a block or two.

It was half an hour before Joe and Eddie returned. "Where's Sam?" Hally cried, but she could see the answer on their faces.

"Can't find him," Joe said, his voice raw and ragged. "He followed the guy, and we never caught up. We lost sight of them around Washington Square."

"We've been hunting all over town," Eddie added. His voice was hoarse also. From calling Sam, Hally guessed. "They could have gone any-where—up Bellevue, down Thames, or even doubled back."

"The jerk!" Jason's face was very red. "Kidnapping Sam—he's not gonna get away with that!"

"No, he's not," Joe agreed. "You can bet your last dollar I'll find my dog."

"We'll get right on it," Hally said. "I've got a map of the town upstairs. We'll split up and cover it all, okay?"

"Yeah," Joe said glumly. He pulled off his glasses and wiped his face on the sleeve of his T-shirt. "And I could use a drink."

Eddie nodded at the paper that Jason held. "That's what he delivered?"

"Yeah." Jason held the message up where the two older boys could see it. "It's the longest one he's ever brought me."

"So he's gone back to silver ink on black paper," muttered Joe.

"Maybe my theory is right," ventured Hally. "There are *two* people sending messages. Ace always delivers his, and his codes are always silver on black. Then there's whoever gave us the bed, who *pretends* to be Ace, and he mails white on black messages."

"But we've seen only one man," Tuyet pointed out.

"Maybe the other sender isn't even a guy!" Eddie said. "What's the code say? Maybe that'll give us a clue about where to find Sam."

"Can't crack it so far," Jason admitted. "It's a new code. Built on the last one, but this one's a brainbuster."

Up on the Watkins's deck, the Casecrackers studied a map of the town. Standing around the picnic table, they refueled on crackers, cheese, and juice while Joe blocked out Newport into four sections.

"What about me?" With a banana half-strangled in one hand and a stub of pencil stuck behind his ear, Jason looked up from his code. "Which section's mine?" He gave Hally a steady glare.

"Your bike wheel's bent," she reminded him.

"And the most important job of all right now is to crack that code. If we can't find Sam, you're our only hope."

Jason thought about that, then nodded solemnly. "Okay."

"And I can trust you to stay alone?" Normally, Hally would never have left Jason on his own. But this was an emergency. And to be extra safe, she'd stop by the Ames's apartment on her way out, and ask Mrs. Ames to keep an eye on him.

Jason nodded again. "Just find him."

"We will," Joe swore.

But he was wrong. The Casecrackers combed the town from First Beach to Fort Adams, from the Common Burying Ground all the way out the causeway to Goat Island. They searched the waterfront, the college campus, Historic Hill and Ocean Drive. They yelled for Sam until they were hoarse, and they described him to everyone they met. But no one had seen a masked man riding a bike with a big golden retriever running alongside him.

Finally, exhausted and heartsick, they met back at the Watkins's. "I can't believe it!" Joe slumped down on the picnic table and dropped his head in his hands.

Tuyet touched his shoulder. "He'll come back."

"I told Officer Swinburne," Hally added. He was their favorite officer on the Newport police force, and he knew just about everything that happened in the town. "He said if he spots Sam, he'll pick him up immediately."

"And I stopped by the station to tell Dad," Eddie said. "By now, every firefighter in Newport knows Sam is missing."

"And I called Mom," said Joe, looking a bit cheered. "She said she'll place an ad in tomorrow's *Loudhailer,* offering a reward."

"So we've got the town locked up tight," Hally told him. "He's probably got Sam inside someplace. But the minute he takes him out for a run, somebody is bound to spot him."

Joe nodded grimly. "I sure hope so."

If he's still in Newport at all, Hally worried. But she didn't voice that fear. From the look on Joe's face, he'd thought it already.

"And now, what about the code?" Tuyet asked.

Jason made a face. "I'm working on it as hard as I can."

That was all the hope that he could give Joe— all the hope any of them could offer. Meanwhile, it was nearing dark. Dog or no dog, their families expected them home.

"We've got to be fresh for the race tomorrow," Eddie pointed out.

Joe shook his head. "I don't want to race. Not without Sam."

No one knew what to say.

"Maybe he'll find his way home tonight." Tuyet offered the hope like a small, fragile gift. "Sam is such a smart dog. He'll know you're missing him."

Joe swallowed hard, and nodded. "I gotta go," he said huskily, and hurried down the stairs. Sad and silent, the others followed a few minutes later. Hally sighed and turned to meet Jason's eyes.

He shrugged. "I'm working just as hard as I can."

"I know." She left him to it and went in to make supper. Their dad would be moonlighting at his second job, where he worked for a caterer. During the school year, Jim Watkins was a high school science teacher in Houston. But when his students took their vacations, he seemed to work twice as hard. At least this summer, what with coming to Newport and meeting Tuyet, Joe, and Eddie—and with Jason in her hair every minute—Hally had no time to miss her father's company.

She chopped vegetables, then grated cheese for homemade pizzas. Jason trudged in from the deck and wandered off to his room, clutching the uncracked code. Hally thought of calling him back to help her cook, then decided against it. Tonight there was nothing more important than his cracking that message.

Using flour tortillas for pizza crusts, she constructed two pizzas for Jason and two for herself. Their dad would eat at the party he was catering and probably bring home fancy leftovers.

When the pizzas were almost done, Hally went down the hall to call Jason. But as she passed their father's bedroom, she paused and cocked her head. From beyond the half-closed door, she could hear a faint, scratchy voice.

"The Viper is coming in one wee-eeee-eeek!" it quavered, tiny and yet somehow awful. The hair stirred at the nape of Hally's neck. "The Viper is coming!" promised the horrible little voice, then it broke into an evil chuckle.

Hally swung the door wide. "Jason!" She glared as he slammed the phone down. "You're pestering Professor Abrams again?"

"The Hyena," Jason corrected her. "Yeah—or at least his answering machine."

"And you're flying back to Iowa next week. You don't think he'll figure out who the Viper is?"

"He's too dumb, dumb, *dumb!*" Jason insisted. His eyes were shiny. "And know what, Hally?" He launched himself in a flying belly flop across their father's bed.

"What?" she said, when he'd stopped bouncing. She wanted to go rub his back, but she knew he'd hate that.

"The Hyena changes his answering machine message 'bout every day. Always has some stupid joke to tell, or sometimes a dumb quote from a book—poetry or something. But this time..." Jason's voice quavered. "This time, Hally, he said, 'We can't come to the phone right now.' We!"

Hally sat beside his feet, and tried to think what to say. She'd always dreamed herself, that someday—someway—their parents would remarry. But it didn't look like her dream was going to come true. She sighed and tickled his toes. "Probably just a slip of the tongue, Jase."

He kicked her hand aside.

She tickled him again. "Or maybe he's got a roommate?"

"Yeah," he growled, "that's just what I'm afrai— Cut that out!"

She smiled and stood. Irritated seemed more like the usual Jason than sad. He rolled over and gave her a ferocious scowl. "Pizza's ready," she said mildly, then went to turn off the oven.

They'd nearly finished eating when the phone rang. Hally ran to answer the kitchen extension and, as she had hoped, it was Joe. "He's home?"

"No." Joe still sounded hoarse. "I was hoping..."

"No," she said gently. "We haven't seen him here." And Sam was smart enough to come upstairs to the deck if he did return here. Especially with the smell of pizza wafting out through the screen door. She drew a deep breath. "Have you thought anymore about...about tomorrow?" The race would be no fun without Joe. She couldn't imagine racing at all without him.

"No..." Joe sounded too tired to think.

Jason put down his slice of pizza. "Listen!"

"Hang on," Hally told Joe, and took the receiver from her ear. "What?" Then she heard it, too. A distant, and familiar, whining! "Joe, hang on a minute," she said, not daring to tell him why. She might have imagined it.

But there was no imagining the outburst of barking that greeted their ears when she and Jason rushed out onto the deck. "Sam—it *is* Sam!" Jason tore down the stairs. Hally peered over the railing, but she couldn't see anything in the dark. "Good boy!" crooned Jason from down below. "Good ol' Sam, you dopey old runaway!"

Hally raced back to the phone. "Guess who we've got here?"

By the time Joe and his parents arrived, Hally

and Jason's father had come home. Hally had left Sam as they'd found him. "He was tied like this?" Mr. Kerry asked. Joe was too busy to speak—his face was buried in Sam's golden ruff.

"Yes." Hally winced as Sam whopped her knees with his tail.

Someone had tied a rope from Sam's collar to the door handle of the Baitmobile, which was parked in their driveway. Beyond her father's head, Hally could see the hulking pieces of the Snoozer Cruiser sticking up from the bed of the truck.

"Strange, isn't it?" Mr. Watkins agreed. "If whoever it was knew Sam, then you'd think he'd have brought him back to the Manor."

"Not if it was Ace who brought him back," said Jason, offering Sam another of the party appetizers that Mr. Watkins had brought back from his catering job. "He probably doesn't know where Joe lives. Or who Sam belongs to. And he picked him up here."

"But if he wanted to kidnap Sam, why bring him back?" Joe wondered, letting his dog go at last. Sam spun and licked his ear. Joe laughed and fended him off.

Hally giggled. "That's why! Who'd want to be kissed by a dog?"

Jason smirked. "Especially now that he's got liver breath!"

"You fed him all that pâté?" groaned Jim Watkins. But Hally could tell that he was too pleased to really care.

And Joe couldn't stop grinning. The Kerrys crammed back into their tiny car. Sam stood across Joe's lap, hanging halfway out the window and seeming to smile a pink-tongued good-bye to them all.

"Race in the morning," Hally reminded Joe.

"Right!" Face to furry face with the retriever, Joe grinned back at her. "Sam and me, we wouldn't miss it for the world!"

When they'd stopped calling good-bye, and

the Kerrys' car was out of sight, the Watkinses sighed happily and headed for the stairs. Lagging behind her family, Hally stopped to knock wood on the Snoozer Cruiser's headboard. "Dream of victory!" she whispered, then went off to bed.

ACE

"Wow, would you look at 'em all!" Jason said as the Baitmobile bumped down the lane to King's Park. The beach and the grassy slope above it were swarming with teams of kids. While parents and families looked on, the crews set out the scraps and junk from which they would build their boats when the crazy race started.

Joe knocked on the truck's back window. When Hally turned, he pointed at a clawfoot bathtub down the beach and grinned. "There's one every year!" he mouthed through the glass.

Jason snorted. "Look at those dopes with the refrigerator box! And beach umbrellas! They're going to use those for sails?"

"This looks like fun," Mr. Watkins said wistfully. "Why isn't there a racing class for adults?"

Eddie leaned around the cab and spoke through the driver's window. "How about near that tree, Mr. Watkins?"

"Fine." He steered the Baitmobile to the free spot. As soon as he had parked the truck, the Casecrackers began unloading the parts of the Snoozer Cruiser. They were running late, because Tuyet had forgotten to set her alarm clock. When they'd arrived to pick her up, they'd found her still in bed. She still yawned every few minutes.

By the time the Casecrackers had set out their materials, race time was almost upon them. A group of men, wearing self-important smiles and blue yachting blazers, marched to race commitee headquarters—a table surrounded by bright flags flapping in the breeze. The tallest man stepped to the microphone there. "Van Zandt's dad," said

Eddie out of the side of his mouth. "You can see where he gets it."

"Welcome to the twenty-fifth running of the Alva Suffern Yacht Club Crazy Race," Commodore Van Zandt said, in a smooth, dignified voice. "Before we begin, let me remind everyone of the rules..."

Joe nudged Hally. "Check it out! The competition."

Everywhere, people were turning to stare. A group of boys marched toward the Casecrackers. On their shoulders they carried two aluminum pipes, each perhaps twenty feet long by a foot in diameter. The pipes cut through the crowd like two gigantic spears. The boys themselves reminded Hally of young warriors. Unlike the other ragtag racers in their goofy T-shirts and cutoffs, this crew was dressed in uniform—red polo shirts, black baseball caps, black shorts. They looked older than the other teams, and there were more of them. She counted seven.

And marching at the head of his crew, with a self-satisfied smirk on his face, came B. Stuyvesant Van Zandt IV.

"Quite an entrance!" said Mr. Watkins, as they dropped their load near the Casecrackers.

"Can anyone read the words on their shirts?" Tuyet asked. Their shirts had something silk-screened across the back, Hally saw, as several of them turned toward the committee stand.

Joe pushed his glasses up his sun-burned nose. "'Ship of Fuels.' Stuyvesant's great granddad made his fortune in oil. Nobody in the family has worked a lick since."

Van Zandt's father was still explaining the rules when Sam let out a playful little bark. Hally turned to see him prance up to a tall black man, about the same age as her father. The man grinned, then bent to scratch the retriever's ears. Sam panted happily and leaned against his knees.

"Who's that?" Hally asked Joe.

"Don't know. Somebody's family, or maybe a reporter. Even the TV stations cover the crazy race." Joe was more worried by the Ship of Fuels. "What do you think it'll be?" he asked Eddie. "A catamaran?"

But there was something familiar about that tall, trim figure. Perhaps she'd seen him around town? The man glanced Hally's way, and she turned her head. Then it hit her, and she looked back. He was circling their building site, inspecting the pieces of the Snoozer Cruiser. A lot of other onlookers were doing the same. "Tuyet!" Hally grabbed her sleeve. "Come with me."

"Hey!" Eddie yelled. "The race is about to start."

"Be right back!" Hally called over her shoulder.

"What is it?" Tuyet asked.

"The bikes!" Hally nodded at the chain-link fence that bordered one side of the park. Half a dozen riders had locked their bikes to its links. "I've got a hunch!"

The third bike from the left was a shiny black mountain bike, and on its fender— "It's Ace!" Tuyet gasped, staring at the playing card that was fastened there. "He's here someplace!"

"He's back there by the Snoozer Cruiser— watching us!"

"You're sure that's him?"

"Sure as shooting, as we say in Texas." His bike was fitted with saddlebags. The nearest bag was only half-buckled. Peeking out from under its top flap was a familiar piece of black wool. Hally grabbed it and pulled. Out came the ski mask that they knew so well! "And I'll prove it." Holding the mask behind her back, Hally marched back to their building site.

Tuyet trotted beside her, her face worried and excited all at once. "Do you think he'll still be there?"

He was. Ace stood next to Mr. Watkins. The two men talked cheerfully while they watched the Casecrackers.

Bam! Down the lawn at the race committee headquarters, Commodore Van Zandt aimed a smoking starting gun at the sky. "Let the race begin," he intoned into the microphone. "Racers, you have two hours to build your vessels."

Everyone cheered, then rushed for their materials. The sounds of hammers, drills, and shouted directions filled the park.

"Step on it!" Joe yelled, motioning for the girls to hurry.

"Half a sec'," Hally called, stopping beside the two men. They turned to smile at her. She smiled back, then whipped the mask from behind her back. "Did you lose something, sir?"

The man looked from the mask, to Hally's face, then back again. All the Casecrackers turned to stare. The man threw back his head and laughed. "Busted!" he said cheerfully, and held out his hand for the mask. "I heard you Casecrackers were good!"

"*You're* the masked rider?" Jason cried. "You're Ace?" He dropped the tape and hurried over.

"That's what my friends call me," the man admitted. He looked at Hally. "But how'd you guess?"

"Sam told me. You two made friends yesterday, right?"

He laughed again, and nodded. "That's right, we had a great—"

"*Hey!*" Eddie yelled, and everyone turned to look. He held a bucket up, then turned it sideways. Blue sky showed through the bucket. Someone had cut a fist-sized hole in its bottom! As everyone gaped, Eddie upended another bucket to show them a similar hole. Then another. "We've been sabotaged! Some creep cut a hole in every last one of our buckets!"

"I didn't check the bottoms when I set them out," murmured Tuyet, looking as if she were near tears. "The lids were still on, and I was so sleepy..."

"That doesn't matter," Hally said. She swung to glare at Ace. "What matters is who would do such a creepy thing, and why?"

Mr. Watkins frowned. "Hally, what are you suggesting?"

"That's not all!" Eddie added. He and Joe were doing a hurried inspection of all the parts of the Snoozer Cruiser. "Somebody's filled all the slots in the bed frame with glue or something. The side-board hooks can't attach to the headboard."

"And get this! Somebody has weakened the headboard and footboard!" Joe reported. "They're sawn almost all the way through, right along the seam with the bedposts, where nobody would notice if they weren't looking for it." He threw down the headboard, and one bedpost snapped off. Sticking his chin out, Joe clenched his hands and marched toward Ace. "You did this, didn't you? You were by the truck last night when you tied Sam to it."

"Now *just* a second, son," Mr. Watkins objected. "Professor Benson teaches at the college here in Newport. Do you really think he'd go around wrecking kids' boats?"

"He's been sending me codes and rattlesnake tails!" Jason said, "So why not?"

"Look," said the professor. He swept all the angry Casecrackers with a serious gaze. "I didn't do this. I know it looks bad. I *was* by the truck last night when I brought Sam back. But anybody could have damaged your bed-boat. It wasn't locked up."

Hally bit her lip. Like her own father, Benson had what she thought of as a "good" face. His eyes met hers straight-on, and he looked as if he smiled more often than he frowned. "You gave us the bed in the first place, didn't you?"

Benson nodded. "I overheard you in the library lobby, the other day, talking about boat designs for the crazy race. I'd just bought myself a waterbed, so I didn't need my old bed anymore.

And I thought you might find it useful." He glanced at her father. "If you kids would excuse me a minute, I'd like to talk to your dad."

Hally shrugged, bewildered. The Casecrackers gathered while the two men stepped aside and talked earnestly. "Doesn't make sense," Joe growled. "To give us the bed, then wreck it?"

"But he sent me the codes!" Jason protested. "He admits it!"

"But the codes never hurt you," Tuyet pointed out. "They were a mystery, but not a mean one."

"Meanwhile, what do we do for a boat?" asked Hally.

"This one's a goner," Eddie said gloomily. "And we've lost ten minutes already. We're out of the race."

Joe kicked up a puff of sand. "And Stuyvesant's building another killer ship. Look at that. No way a kid designed that one. And those pipes alone cost way more than twenty-five dollars. He's bending the rules as usual."

The Ship of Fuels crew was working intently. The two pipes had been laid side by side, about ten feet apart. Four pointed aluminum caps turned them into watertight tubes. Two smaller pipes made an X to join the big pipes. Stout rope tied it all together.

"Gonna be a catamaran," Eddie confirmed. "It'll be fast."

Mr. Watkins and Professor Benson rejoined them. "Kids," said Mr. Watkins, his face serious. "Professor Benson has explained the situation to me. He can't tell you right now, but he has a very good reason for what he's done. And he didn't sabotage your boat. You'll just have to trust me on this, for now."

Hally knew how *she* felt, but she looked at the other Casecrackers. One by one, they nodded. "We believe you, then," she said at last. "And I'm sorry for even thinking it."

The professor smiled. "Apology accepted. I'd probably have thought the same, under the circumstances. So now, how are you Casecrackers going to win this race?"

Hally looked at Eddie, who shrugged. But she wasn't going to give up, even if he had. "We'll just have to design a new boat. Who knows where we can find a lot of junk in one place?"

"That's easy," said the professor. "My basement's full of junk."

"Then let's go get it!" Hally and Jason's father led the charge to the Baitmobile. Hally and the two adults scrambled into the cab, and the other Casecrackers piled in the back.

As they backed out of the park, they passed by the Ship of Fuels. Stuyvesant looked up and smirked at them. "*Quitting* so soon?" he jeered. "You'd let a few lousy little holes stop you?"

"You did it!" Jason howled from the back of the truck. "How else would you know our buckets had holes?"

Stuyvesant grinned. "Gee, I dunno. Lucky guess?"

"If he were ten years older..." Mr. Watkins growled, and the professor nodded grimly.

Glaring at Stuyvesant as the truck drove slowly past, Hally saw something gray hit his shirt. It splattered to make a stain the size of a plate!

Stuyvesant looked down at his chest in shock. Then, as he smelled what had hit him, his nose wrinkled in disgust. He looked up just in time to see a second dead fish sailing head over tailfins toward him! He ducked, and it skated through his hair. He let out a furious howl and wiped at his blond hair with both hands.

"A rotten fish for a fish-brained cheater!" Jason taunted as they rolled away. He'd found his ammunition in the bucketful of week-old lobster bait—the smellier, the better, Joe's cousin had explained to them—that was tucked into a back corner of the Baitmobile's bed.

"Jason, you cut that out!" Mr. Watkins called out his window. But he was choking with laughter.

In the back, laughing so hard they could barely move, Eddie and Joe were clamping the lid back on the bait bucket. A giggling Tuyet banished Jason to the tail end of the truck. After handling the bait, he smelled as ripe as Van Zandt.

Hally watched as Sam sniffed Jason, then rubbed his shoulder on him to share in the glorious smell. Jason hugged the retriever. Then his eyes met Hally's through the glass. Brother and sister shared a wide grin and a thumbs-up.

The Baitmobile reached pavement and set off with a roar.

THE CRAZY RACE

"He's got spunk!" The professor laughed, also looking back at Jason. "Has he cracked his latest code yet?"

"No, but he will." Hally looked at the professor. "You really won't tell why you've been bringing him those codes all summer?"

"I can't, Hally," he said. But he said it nicely.

She wrinkled her nose. "Then...could you tell me why you sent him a rattlesnake rattle? That really spooked us."

The professor smiled. "Sorry about that. I think it was meant to intrigue, not to scare."

That's a funny way to put it, Hally thought.

He thinks...But if he sent it, doesn't he know?

They bumped shoulders as the Baitmobile turned a corner and shot up the hill. Jim Watkins was taking a shortcut that led behind a grocery store. A dumpster stood next to the building, and it was filled to the brim with— "Stop!" Hally yelled. "Those boxes, that's it! *There's* our boat!"

The Baitmobile squealed to a halt, and her dad stared at her. "What are you talking about?"

Bursting with excitement, Hally explained.

Minutes later, the Baitmobile raced back to King's Park. In back, Tuyet, Eddie, and Joe were buried to their chins in boxes that had once held bananas. Sam was squished up against the back window. Jason sat on Hally's lap and bounced with joy. "It's gonna work, it's gonna work!" he crowed. "Hally, you're almost as smart as I am!"

The professor and Mr. Watkins laughed. Jason turned to the professor. "So what I want to know is, how come you changed the pattern halfway through?"

"How do you mean?"

"All the codes were silver ink on black paper, and hand delivered. Till you mailed me the white and black one about the bed in the basement."

The professor nodded. "After I overheard you in the library, I knew you needed a boat—and soon. It was quicker to mail the message, because I can only drop by to deliver codes one or two days a week—"

Jason nodded smugly. "Yeah, I figured that out."

"I teach classes the other days. That's why I was so slow bringing Sam back. I had to give a summer school final exam, and I was late already. Sam followed me to class. I wasn't sure he knew his way home, so I kept him with me till I could deliver him safely."

"But why'd you change the color of the codes?" Jason insisted. "Then you changed back again for this one."

"Crack it and you'll know," said the professor.

"Well, tell me this."

"This is your last question, Jase," warned Mr. Watkins.

"Tell me why you're called Ace? And why does your bike wear a playing card?"

The professor chuckled. He and Mr. Watkins exchanged what Hally thought of as "grown-up" looks. "Because I was in the Air Force once upon a time," the professor said. "My father was a fighter pilot in an all-black squadron during World War II, and I followed in his footsteps. Friends started calling me 'Ace,' and I had it painted on the side of my plane."

Jason gave a hop on Hally's lap. "You were a pilot? An ace?"

He chuckled at Jason's excitement. "Yep. Still am, for that matter. But nowadays, I fly a little single-engine plane."

"Wooooow," Jason crooned. And then they were at King's Park, and there was no time left to talk. They had eighty minutes until race time.

The Ship of Fuels crew was just carrying its vessel down to the water. Stuyvesant looked surprised to see them, then angry. But then he ignored them.

The Casecrackers flung the boxes out of the truck. Mr. Watkins, the professor, and Sam drove off for another load, and the Casecrackers gathered around Hally. "It's very simple." She held up one of the boxes of black garbage bags that they'd bought at the grocery store after they'd found the banana boxes. "Two banana boxes should fit in each garbage bag. Squeeze all the air out of each bag, then fasten it tight. The bag will make the boxes watertight, so they'll float. Then we'll stack the two-box units together till they make one great big box. Let's make it about as wide and long as a double mattress. And about as tall as Jason."

"*That's* not very tall," Eddie noted without cracking a smile. Jason glared.

"But tall enough," Hally said. "Then, once we

have that giant box, we'll use our tape and string
to tie it together. Like an enormous, waterproof
Christmas package."

The Casecrackers set to work. As they finished, the Baitmobile returned with more boxes.
"Fifty minutes left," Eddie warned. They started
a second gigantic cube, while the truck went off
for more. They finished this box even faster, now
that they knew what to do. "Thirty-five," said
Eddie, as the truck returned.

Working frantically, they made the third box
in fifteen minutes flat. "Twenty minutes till race
time," said Eddie. "Now what?"

"We tie the three cubes together," said Hally.
"They'll be like three boxcars. We slide the mast
down between the front box and the middle
box, and we tie it there. You're in charge of
that, Eddie."

He nodded. "We'll stay it by tying ropes from
the mast top to ropes on the second box. That
should work."

"Great!" Hally turned. "Joe, why don't you get to work on your rudder? Figure out some way to attach it to the caboose box."

He grinned. "Easy enough—ropes."

Hally and the others set to work connecting all three boxcars. The boxes looked as if some crazy spider had tried to web them with ropes and tape. Once the boxes were linked, the Case-crackers laid down the deck—the sheet of plywood from the Snoozer Cruiser—and tied it in place with twine laced through its screw holes. "That'll spread the load, so we don't put a foot through cardboard," Eddie said approvingly. He checked his watch. "Four minutes. We've got to launch this thing."

"But will she sail?" worried Joe.

Eddie shrugged. "She'll float, and it's all downwind from here. What more can I say?"

"Racers, you have three minutes to reach the starting line," the commodore announced over the loudspeaker.

Up and down the beach, friends and family were helping the racers put to sea. Bathtubs were lifted and barrels were rolled. One craft broke in half when its crew lifted it. "Half the fleet will sink before they reach the starting line," Eddie predicted. "It's the same every year."

With the help of Mr. Watkins and Professor Ace, as they were starting to call him, the Casecrackers hoisted their banana-box boat. Shrouded in its shiny black plastic, and with its blue tarp junk sail, it made Hally think of a lumpy, gift-wrapped dragon. Jason had fastened his Halloween mask to the front of the mast. It gave the "Bananaboat" a foolishly fierce look. *Look out Stuyvesant, here we come,* she thought proudly.

Fifty feet out, the racers who had stayed afloat were anchored near the committee boat, a small powerboat flying nautical race flags. A quarter mile beyond the starting line, Hally could see the two orange balls that marked the finish line.

They set the Bananaboat down in the cool shallows—it floated! In fact, it floated so high that Professor Ace and Mr. Watkins had to give everyone a leg up, including Sam. The Casecrackers scrambled aboard and took their positions.

"Be fast," Jim Watkins advised, as Eddie took the tiller.

"And watch out for your pal," added the professor, nodding at Stuyvesant's distant, sleek catamaran. "I'd bet he's still in a snit."

POW! On the committee boat, a standing figure held a smoking gun. "We're late!" Jason groaned.

"But we're not beat yet," said Eddie. The Bananaboat started to pick up speed. "We've got a lot of windage."

"That's bad?" asked Tuyet.

"Nope. Since the wind's blowing the right direction, that's good." The Bananaboat wallowed past an overturned craft. This one was an old sofa with a couple of foam logs tied underneath. Its crew was paddling around in life jackets, trying to turn it upright again. "Look at Stuyvesant go," growled Joe.

The catamaran was out in front of everyone. Unlike the other boats, this one moved with speed and grace. "It looks like a real boat," Hally muttered.

"And that's the whole point," Eddie agreed. "This is a race for homemade boats. Some professional designed that one, or I'll eat a banana box. Hally, ease your sheets, okay?"

"Uh oh!" Joe said suddenly. "He's tacking. He's headed back this way."

Eddie shook his head. "That jerk! He figures his boat's fast enough to let him come back and rag on us and still win the race."

"And look what he's got," Joe said.

"A slingshot!" Eddie cried. "They're totally illegal."

Closer and closer to the clumsy Bananaboat

glided the Ship of Fuels. Its crew was seated on the trampoline deck—a piece of canvas laced tight between the pipes. Two boys were stretching back a gigantic sling.

"Heads up!" Eddie yelled.

On the catamaran, the sling snapped forward. Something round and white flew toward them. It smacked into the water between the boats, and seawater showered the Casecrackers. "Water balloon," said Joe. "But it'll hurt plenty if it hits you, moving at that speed."

The cat' glided closer and closer. Aboard it, the marksmen pulled back their sling.

"Yah! Fishbait!" screamed Jason, standing to shake his fist. "You've got bait breath, fish eyes, scaly skin, and the brain of a flounder! You and your grandmother couldn't hit the broad side of a—"

WHAM! The water balloon crashed into the side of the Bananaboat and exploded, spraying them all. Jason fell over. Tuyet pounced on him before he rolled off the deck and into the water.

Hooting and jeering, Stuyvesant and his crew looked back as they swooped past. "That'll teach you some manners, you smart-mouth runt!" Stuyvesant yelled. "And as for *you*, townie girl—" The catamaran stopped dead in the water. Its mast swayed forward alarmingly. The crew fell down and landed in a yelping mass.

"Hooo!" Eddie whooped, and jumped for joy. "Why don't you watch where you're sailing, big shot?" Cackling, he thumbed his nose at the cat' and its crew.

"What happened?" cried Hally. "Why'd they stop like that?"

Joe was also laughing. "The jerks ran over a mooring buoy! It's probably jammed in their crossbars."

"So long, suckers!" Eddie called. "See ya at the finish line!" The rich snob was glaring after them while his crew worked to free the cat'.

Jason stuck his thumbs in his ears and waggled

his fingers. "So lo-oong, Fishbait!" he taunted. "He who laughs last—"

Stuyvesant dived off the cat' and set after them.

"Wow!" said Hally. "He's really mad!"

"Can't stand to lose," muttered Joe. "Will he catch us, Ed?"

Eddie looked back, looked forward, and said, "Port sheets come in a foot. Starboard out the same, Tuyet. That's all we can do."

It wasn't enough. Stuyvesant sliced through the water after them, his face grim and determined.

"What's he gonna do?" Jason worried.

"He's got a knife!" Tuyet squealed, her eyes wide.

A few yards behind the slow-moving boat, Stuyvesant stopped to tread water. He held up his pocket knife.

"Put your knife away, and keep off," Joe warned. "Are you nuts?"

"Laugh at me, will you? Let's see you laugh at *this!*" Stuyvesant glided to the stern of the Bananaboat and caught its rudder. Then he jabbed his knife into the boxes!

"Let go, you creep!" Eddie yelled, wrenching at the tiller while he slid one leg over the side of the Bananaboat to kick at Stuyvesant.

Hally wished she had a paddle to smack him with! She and the others yelled insults at him, and Sam was barking furiously. The boat sat so high in the water that they could barely reach their attacker. Stuyvesant kept dodging Eddie's kicks, and everyone else's too, as he moved along the back of the boat, stabbing boxes. Then he ducked underwater, and they could feel the blows of the knife.

"Where's the committee boat?" Tuyet cried, her eyes bright with tears of rage.

"Over on the far side." Joe's face was white and his voice shook. "They'll never see him from that distance."

As water filled the boxes in the rear of the boat, the Bananaboat started to settle. Its majestic glide slowed to a crawl.

Stuyvesant came up for air. He swiped the blond hair out of his eyes and smirked up at them. "Most townie boats sink in every crazy race. What a shame." Swimming closer, he attacked the back boxes on the other side.

This time Joe's kick grazed their attacker's head as he swam past. Stuyvesant grabbed Joe's foot and tried to pull him into the water.

"You wait until we get back to shore," Eddie swore. "You're dead meat."

Jason yanked the rubber mask off the mast. "You crummy, lousy creep!" Hanging off the edge of the deck, he swatted Stuyvesant again and again in the back of the head with the mask. "Get away from us! Get *away!*"

Stuyvesant raised a hand to fend him off, and the mask hit his knife. The knife plopped into the water and sank. "Hey!" Stuyvesant glared up at him. Then his glare turned to a sneer, and he shrugged. "Oh well, guess I've done enough for one day. Happy sinking, townies!" He turned and swam off toward his cat'.

And Sam took a flying leap off the Bananaboat! Smacking into the water, he set after the swimmer! "Get him, Sam!" screamed Jason.

"Sam. Come back here, boy!" Joe yelled.

But Sam paddled onward, golden head darting with each stroke. He was gaining!

And they were sinking. The back third of the Bananaboat was half underwater. Hally looked around desperately. They just *couldn't* end the race like this! Then it hit her. "Let's cut off her caboose! Joe, you have a knife, don't you?"

"So do I!" Eddie pulled his from a pocket. "What do we do?"

"He only stabbed the boxes in the back cube. That's what's slowing us down! If we cut it away, would she still sail?"

Eddie's face lit up. "She'll sail, or she'll do a somersault if the mast overbalances her."

"Let's try it then!" Joe was cutting already—slashing the ropes that attached the rear box to the middle one. Hally took Eddie's knife and helped, while Eddie stayed at the tiller. Tuyet and Jason untied the twine that held the plywood deck in place. They'd slide it forward when they cast off the sinking caboose.

Meanwhile, Eddie looked over his shoulder and laughed. "Sam's got him!"

Everyone turned to see. Sam had caught hold of the back of Stuyvesant's shirt. He was trying to retrieve the snob—drag him back to the Bananaboat! Stuyvesant was splashing and yelling. And making no headway at all toward his own boat. He tried to push Sam away, but Sam held him too tightly.

"Way to go, Sam!" Jason cheered.

Joe cut away the rudder, and dragged it alongside the middle cube. "We'll have to hold it in place. No time to tie it," he gasped.

As Hally finished cutting the last of the connecting lines, Joe whistled for Sam. "Sam, here boy!"

This time Sam obeyed. He let go of the struggling swimmer and turned. Shoulders pumping, brown eyes gleeful, he surged after the Bananaboat. "We're picking up steam!" Eddie reported. "Tell that hound to step on it."

To rescue Sam, the Casecrackers had to dangle Hally over the back. Eddie and Jason held her ankles, Tuyet her belt. When she caught Sam's scruff, she pulled him high enough for Joe to grab hold. Somehow they dragged everyone back aboard. Then they all stayed at the very back of the Bananaboat to counterbalance the weight of the mast.

Joe sat up, panting. "Is the cat' free yet?"

"Looks like nearly," Eddie muttered. "But they're facing the wrong way from Van Zandt. Ooops! They're off. Ha!"

The catamaran was sailing again—*away* from Stuyvesant. They could hear him yelling. But he couldn't catch up. And whoever was steering the craft clearly did not know how to sail her. The cat' tacked twice, but it couldn't seem to circle back to its captain.

Jason looked forward. "What about the rest of the racers?"

They were spread out all over the course. Few were making much headway, and a couple were sinking. Perhaps a hundred feet ahead, something that looked sort of like a canoe, but with a paddle wheel and an umbrella, wobbled toward the finish line. Just behind it, a girl sat astride a fifty-gallon barrel with outriggers. Its sail was a flowered sheet fastened to a pole that the girl held upright.

"Gonna be close," Eddie said. "A hundred yards to the finish. And here comes the committee boat, now that we don't need them."

The boat roared past, headed for Stuyvesant,

who was still chasing his catamaran.

The wind gusted, and the junk rig swayed wildly. Everyone shrieked as the Bananaboat rolled and nearly turned turtle! "Everybody lie down!" Eddie snapped. "Get your weight low!" The boat settled again on its course. Looking over the side at the water, Hally could see that they were moving faster.

"Southwester's coming up," Eddie noted. "If it holds and we don't tip..."

"They picked him up," Joe reported, looking back. The committee boat had taken Stuyvesant aboard and was chasing the cat'.

"That's not fair!" Tuyet protested.

The Bananaboat wallowed past the girl on the barrel. She laughed and waved. Now there was only the canoe-thing between them and the finish.

"They've put him aboard," Eddie growled, looking back. "That boat's so fast, he might still—"

Looking back, Hally saw Stuyvesant scramble into position. He wrenched the tiller from his friend. The committee boat was drawing away, while the catamaran tacked. As she watched, it picked up speed—then it jerked to the left.

"Dodging a mooring buoy," said Joe, then "Oh— Wow!"

Intent on its course for another sinking boat, the committee boat zigged as the catamaran zagged. Somebody yelled. A horrible, crunching thump sounded across the water, along with cries of outrage—the cat' had rammed the committee boat!

"I love it, I love it, I *love* it!" At the tiller, Eddie jigged for joy.

Joe was laughing so hard that he choked— Hally had to thump his back. She and Tuyet and Jason couldn't stop giggling.

And the Bananaboat glided on past the canoe-thing—to win the crazy race by half a length!

CHAPTER 11

THE MYSTERIOUS CODES

"I wish you guys weren't leaving next week,"
Joe said, as he handed Hally a hot dog. It was
early evening and they stood on the Watkins's
second-floor deck. In the backyard below, the
other Casecrackers, their parents, and friends
stood laughing and talking around the Ames's
barbecue grill. To celebrate the victory in the
crazy race that day, Jim Watkins was throwing
an end-of-summer party.

"Me too," Hally admitted. "I'll sure miss you
all when we go back to Texas. And I'll miss
being a Kerry Hill Casecracker."

Tuyet had joined them while Hally spoke.

"You *can't* leave before we've cracked our last case!" she protested. "We still don't know why Professor Ace is sending Jason the codes."

Hally nodded. "Let's go see if Jason has cracked his last message," she suggested. "Maybe when he does that, we'll know."

Jason sprawled on a blanket near the grill. With a pencil tucked behind his ear and a battered hot dog clutched in one hand, he was glaring down at a sheet of scribbled figures and numbers. Sam crouched beside him and stared at his hot dog.

"How's it going?" Joe asked, as he, Hally, and Tuyet sat down on the blanket.

"It's weird," Jason growled. "All I know is it's numbers for letters, like last time. But nothing works." He bit off an enormous bite of hot dog and frowned while he chewed it.

"The crazy race champs!" Professor Ace saluted them as he, Eddie, and Mr. Watkins strolled over. They'd left Chief Machado in charge of the grill. Smoke rising around him, he waved a long fork and looked right at home.

"Cracked it yet?" asked Jim Watkins.

Jason shook his head. "It's these stupid zeroes." He turned the black paper so that his dad and the professor could see the first part of the message.

15.0000. 10.00.00.16.000.11.5. 0. 17.000.12.00.14.
18.0000.00000.9.3. 1.00.
12.00000.14.00. 3.00.9.000.5.6.16!

"See? Zero, or zero-zero, or zero-zero-zero. Or four zeroes. Or five. I'm sick of stupid zeroes!"

Mr. Watkins rubbed his chin. "So there's five ways of writing zero?" he said after a minute.

"Yeah." Jason looked frustrated. He wasn't used to codes he couldn't crack.

"And those five kinds of zeroes stand for letters," his dad added, meaningfully. When Jason simply shrugged, he asked, "What five letters go together, son?"

Jason's lips formed an O. "Vowels!" he yelped.

"There are only five vowels! Why didn't I think of—" He dropped his hot dog, grabbed his pencil and started scribbling.

"It ain't gonna be the same without you guys," Eddie said, while Jason worked. "Are you sure you're coming back next summer?"

Hally felt like crying. She was missing Newport and her friends, and she hadn't even left yet! And she'd miss Jason, too, pest that he was, when he flew back to Iowa. "Dad?" she appealed.

"How'd you feel," he countered, "if we didn't go back to Texas at all? Ace tells me that the college has an opening in the science department, where he teaches. I thought I might apply."

"How'd I *feel?*" Hally sat straight up. "You mean we could stay in Newport?"

"Only if I get the job," her dad said hastily.

"You'll get it, Jim," Ace spoke up. "You're more than qualified. And I'll put in a word with the head of the department."

"All riiiight!" Eddie chortled. He slapped a low five with Joe, who passed it on to Tuyet. Giggling, she passed it to Hally, who slapped Professor Ace's palm.

It went right around the circle to Jason, who sighed and broke the chain. "Yeah, you get to stay here and be a Casecracker," he told Hally. "I've gotta go back and watch that stupid Hyena drool all over Mom. It's no fair!"

Eddie sniggered. "And you'd better hope he never guesses who's been sending him those spooky Viper letters!"

Jim Watkins frowned. He was about to say, "What Viper letters?" Hally could tell.

But before he could, Professor Ace cleared his throat. "Figured that code out yet?" he asked Jason.

"Getting there," Jason grumbled. "There's more double zeroes than anything else. And everybody knows that there's more *E*s than any other vowel in English." He held up his scratch sheet so the others could see the simple key he had printed out. "So if *E* equals *00*, and you write the vowels like this..."

A E I O U
OO

"Then A probably equals *0*," Joe concluded.

"And *I* is *000*," said Tuyet. "And so on!"

"Right," Jason said, looking happier. He quickly printed the alphabet.

"Now, if my mysterious coder did what he's done every other time, he built this code on his last one," he continued, printing a row of numbers below the letters. "So what if, since *A* already has a number—*0*—then *B* equals *1* this time?"

"I get it!" said Hally. "Then *C* equals *2*, *D* equals *3*..."

"You skip *E*, since it's a vowel," agreed Jason. "That makes *F* equal *4*, and so on." He printed the numbers out, making a key to decode the message.

```
   O       OO      OOO
  A B C D E F G H  I  J K L M
   1 2 3     4 5 6     7 8 9 10
 OOOO              OOOOO
 N O P Q R S  T U V W Z Y Z
 11  12 13 14 15 16  17 18 19 20 21
```

"When you crack the code, it will be another line of the poem," Tuyet predicted. "Because it doesn't make sense yet. It can't be finished." She closed her eyes and recited the lines that had been sent to Jason, one by one, all summer long. "'Things that go bump in the night...Well, they never give me a fright...'"

The other Casecrackers joined in. "'As for snakes, well, I've met them...And sometimes I've et them...'" They looked at Jason expectantly.

His pencil flew over the black paper of his latest code. One by one, he filled in the meaning of each silver letter.

"'So...meeting...a...V...I...P...'" He paused, his eyes rounding. "'So meeting a VIPER would...be...pure...delight!'" He gulped, and looked up at them. "Viper! That means…"

"The only person who could guess you're the Viper, besides us, is the person you sent your Viper letters to," Hally said.

"The Hyena!" Jason cried. "You mean it's been the stupid *Hyena* who's been…" His eyes filled with angry tears. "He's known all *summer* it was me?" His voice squeaked, and his face flushed brick red. He clamped his arms tight around his knees, and suddenly he looked very small and very miserable.

Jim Watkins started to touch his shoulder, then didn't. He glanced at Ace, as if for help.

"How did you come to help the Hye—umm—Professor Abrams, then?" Hally asked Ace, who also looked worriedly at Jason.

"We went to graduate school together, out in the Midwest," he said. "Hiram and I were—still are—best friends. He called and asked me to deliver the codes, Jason. He mailed his coded messages to me, then I brought them to you."

"Professor Abrams couldn't mail them directly to Jason, because we'd have seen the Iowa postmark and guessed who was sending them," Hally reasoned.

"But why'd you wear the ski mask and gloves and all?" Eddie demanded.

Professor Ace smiled. "Newport's a small town. I figured you'd be watching for me after my first couple of deliveries. And if you knew what I looked like, you might spot me around town later on and demand an explanation."

"It was much more mysterious, with you wearing a mask," Tuyet assured him.

He laughed. "Well, we aim to please!"

"And that's why the codes changed color," Joe realized. "Because the black on white code— about the bed in your basement—came from you, not Professor Abrams."

"See?" Hally said, nudging him with her elbow. "I *told* you there had to be two code senders!"

"Right again." Ace grinned. "I didn't have any of Hiram's silver ink. So I wrote my message in black, on white paper. But I wrote it in Hiram's code."

"He knew all along!" Jason muttered, his chin still on his knees. "He's been laughing at me all summer. What a jerk I am!"

Ace dropped a hand on his knee. "Hiram hasn't been laughing at you, son," he said firmly. "He's just been giving as good as he got. You were trying to scare him with those Viper letters, weren't you? Would *you* take that lying down—from anybody?"

Jason didn't look comforted. "No, but..."

"You've still got a lot of his message to decode," said Mr. Watkins. "Maybe you should see what else he has to say."

"Who cares?" But Jason picked up his pencil and hunched over his code.

"Hiram's a good guy," Ace said, though Jason ignored him. "I don't know how serious he and your mother are, but if things work out that way, he'd make a great father. And a good friend." His dark eyes swung to Jim Watkins, and they looked at each other, unsmiling.

Hally realized that some kind of message had passed between the two men. Her dad gave a short, jerky nod, then turned to Jason. "What's the rest of the message, Jase?"

Jason wrinkled his nose, then turned the message that he'd been printing out, so that they could read it.

> **BY THE WAY, MR. VIPER, I'M GOING TO A RATTLE-SNAKE ROUNDUP DOWN IN NEW MEXICO NEXT MONTH. WANT TO COME WITH ME AND SEE SOME REAL VIPERS? (IF YOUR MOM'S NICE TO US, MAYBE WE'LL BRING HER ALONG—WHAT DO YOU THINK?) MEANWHILE, LOOKING FORWARD TO THE VIPER'S COMING,**
>
> **YOURS IN HERPETOLOGY,**
> **HIRAM ABRAMS**

Jason looked less unhappy as he looked up from the message. "What's herp—um—herpetology?"

"The study of snakes," said Mr. Watkins. He glanced at Ace. "Abrams is a herpetologist?"

Ace nodded. "A real, sure 'nough snake man."

"I never knew that!" Jason's eyes were starting to gleam.

"If he takes you on a rattler roundup, you wear your high boots," Ace warned him with a faint grin. "'Cause if I know Hiram, you won't be *watching* vipers, you'll be out there in the bushes *bagging* them!"

"Yow!" Jason muttered. "Yow's-a-mighty!"

Mr. Watkins dropped an arm around his shoulders. "Doesn't sound so bad, does it?" he asked, giving him a brief hug. "And when you're not busy having fun with your mom and Professor Abrams in Iowa," he added huskily, "you'll be here in Newport, having fun with Hally and me."

"And cracking cases," Hally reminded him. "'Cause you're a Kerry Hill Casecracker, and don't you forget it!"

"Yeah," said Jason, starting to smile.

"But right now, you just lost your hot dog." Tuyet pointed at Sam, whose furry muzzle was smeared with ketchup. Brown eyes hopeful, he stood and wagged his tail.

Hally laughed and stood too. "Okay, Case-crackers, who's ready for seconds?"

"I am!" Jason bounced to his feet and led the charge to the grill.

THE **KeRRy** HILL

CASECRACKERS

*Join the Kerry Hill Casecrackers
for each one of these adventures:*

ABOUT THE AUTHORS

The authors of The Kerry Hill Casecrackers are Peggy Nicholson and John F. Warner. A native Texan, a graduate of Brown University, and a former high school art teacher, Nicholson has been writing and living in Newport for the past several years. The author of several Harlequin novels, she was twice a finalist for the Golden Medallion, awarded for the best romance novel of the year. She has also published plays and short stories in textbook anthologies and has written several books for young readers.

A former teacher, editor, and publishing executive, Warner is the founder of a Newport business that creates and produces educational materials and children's books. He is also the author of more than 70 short stories, plays, and nonfiction pieces that appear in a variety of anthologies. He has written hundreds of magazine and newspaper articles, as well as several books for Lerner Publications Company.